Praise for Jennifer L. Armentrout:

Standalone novels:

'A drum-tight sense of suspense and sexual tension'
Publishers Weekly on *The Return*

'Sizzling, forbidden romance and non-stop action make
The Return an addictive read. Sign me up for the sequel – I
am now officially a Seth-a-holic!' Jeaniene Frost, *New York
Times* bestselling author

The Lux series:

'An action-packed ride that will leave you breathless and
begging for more' Jus Accardo, author of *Touch*

'Powerful. Addictive' *Winter Haven Books*

'A thrilling ride from start to finish' *RT Book Reviews*

'Witty, refreshing and electrifying' *Shortie Says*

'Fast-paced and entertaining ... I couldn't put this one
down' *YA Fantasy Guide*

'An engrossing, sexy nail-biter!' Nanny Holder, author of
Wicked

Jennifer L. Armentrout lives in West Virginia. All the rumors you've heard about her state aren't true. Well, mostly. When she's not hard at work writing, she spends her time reading, working out, watching zombie movies, and pretending to write. She shares her home with her husband, his K-9 partner named Diesel, and her hyper Jack Russell Loki. Her dreams of becoming an author started in algebra class, where she spent her time writing short stories . . . therefore explaining her dismal grades in math. Jennifer writes Adult and Young Adult Urban Fantasy and Romance.

Find out more at www.jenniferarmentrout.com
Follow her on Twitter @JLArmentrout
or find her on Facebook/JenniferLArmentrout

Also by Jennifer L. Armentrout
and available from Hodder:

The Covenant Series
Daimon (novella)
Half-Blood
Pure
Deity
Elixir (novella)
Apollyon
Sentinel

The Lux Series
Shadows (novella)
Obsidian
Onyx
Opal
Origin
Opposition

Standalone Titles
Cursed
Don't Look Back
Unchained (Nephilim Rising)
Obsession
The Return

The Gamble Brothers Series
Tempting the Best Man
Tempting the Player
Tempting the Bodyguard

JENNIFER L. ARMENTROUT

Tempting the
Best Man

A Gamble Brothers Novel

HODDER

Tempting the Best Man first published in eBook in the United States of America in 2012 by Entangled Publishing, LLC

This paperback edition first published in Great Britain in 2015
by Hodder & Stoughton
An Hachette UK company

1

A CIP catalogue record for this title is available from the British Library

Paperback ISBN 978 1 473 61594 6
eBook ISBN 978 1 444 79851 7

Typeset by Hewer Text UK Ltd, Edinburgh
Printed and bound by Clays St Ives plc

Hodder & Stoughton policy is to use papers that are natural, renewable
and recyclable products and made from wood grown in sustainable forests.
The logging and manufacturing processes are expected to conform
to the environmental regulations of the country of origin.

Hodder & Stoughton Ltd
Carmelite House
50 Victoria Embankment
London
EC4Y 0DZ

www.hodder.co.uk

Chapter One

The ivory invitation with its elegant calligraphy and lacy embellishments felt more like a humiliation time bomb just waiting to blow up in Madison Daniels's face than a beautiful wedding announcement. Man, did she have a problem.

Mitch, her big brother by three years—her only brother—was actually getting married this weekend. *Married.*

She was totally happy for him. Thrilled, even. His fiancée, Lissa, was a great gal, and they'd become quick friends. Lissa would never do her brother wrong. A Hallmark movie could be based on the two. Met freshman year at University of Maryland, fell madly in love, got great corporate jobs straight out of college, and the rest was history.

No, Mitch and Lissa weren't the problem.

And a wedding held deep in Northern Virginia's vineyards definitely wasn't the problem.

Not even her semi-lunatic parents, who owned and operated a very profitable online store called DOOMSDAY "R" US and would likely be hawking gas masks to the guests, were the problem. In fact, she'd take an asteroid with "Earth's My Bitch" emblazoned on it and headed her way over this.

Her gaze dropped to the invitation, down to the list of attending bridesmaids and groomsmen, and she winced. She blew out a slow breath, stirring the long strands of brown hair that had escaped her messy twist.

Right across from her name, separated by a few innocent dots and written in crimson ink, was the name of the best man: Chase Gamble.

God hates me. That was it. Well, she was the maid of honor, and any of the other Gamble brothers would've been fine as best man. But oh no, it had to be Chase Gamble. He was her older brother's best friend, confidante, homie, whatever—and otherwise known as the bane of Madison's existence.

"Staring at the invitation isn't going to change a damn thing." Bridget Rodgers leaned a plump hip against Madison's desk, drawing her attention. Her assistant was a study in how a fashion disaster on some people could work for others. Today, Bridget wore a fuchsia pencil skirt paired with a purple peasant shirt sporting large polka dots. A black scarf and leather boots completed the look. Mysteriously, she actually looked good in what should have been a clown's costume. Bridget was bold.

Madison sighed. She could use a little bold right now. "I don't think I can deal with this."

"Look, you should've taken my advice and invited Derek from the history department. At least then you'd be having wild monkey sex instead of lusting after your brother's best friend during the whole wedding. A man who's already rejected you once, might I add."

Bridget had a point. She was crafty like that. "What am I

going to do?" Madison asked, glancing out the window of her office. All she could see was the steel and cement of the museum next to her building—the Smithsonian, which always made her chest swell with pride. She'd worked hard to become one of the privileged few who got to work for this amazing cultural institution.

Bridget leaned down into Madison's face and caught her attention again. "You're going to put on your big-girl panties and deal with it. You may have a secret, undying love for Chase Gamble, but if he hasn't recognized your awesomeness by now the man is clearly mental and so not worth this angst."

"I know, I know," Madison said. "But he's just so . . . *infuriating.*"

"Most men are, sweetie." Bridget winked.

"It's fine he's not interested in me. Disappointing, but I can deal. And I can even forgive him for changing his mind the one time we almost hooked up. Well, sort of." She laughed without much humor and stared at her best friend, willing her to understand. "But he's constantly poking at me, you know? Teasing me in front of my family, treating me like a kid sister, when all I want to do is shake him . . . and get him naked."

"It's just one weekend—how bad can it be?" Bridget asked. She was trying to add the voice of reason to what was going to be the worst weekend of Madison's life.

Dropping the invitation on her desk, she leaned back in her chair and sighed, idly contemplating calling the history department.

Ever since she could remember, there was Chase. Always

Chase. They'd grown up on the same block in the suburbs of DC. Her brother and Chase had been inseparable since, well, forever. Which meant, being the baby of the family, Madison had nothing better to do as a kid than follow behind Mitch and his friends.

She'd idolized Chase. It was hard not to with his masculine beauty, easy candor, and downright illegal dimples. As a boy and into adulthood, Chase had a fierce protective streak that could make a girl's heart do a little flutter in her chest. He was the type of guy who would rip off his shirt in the middle of Snowmageddon and give it to a homeless person on the street, but there'd always been this raw, dangerous edge to him.

Chase wasn't the kind of guy anyone messed with.

Once in high school, a boy had gotten a little too frisky with her in his car parked outside her parents' house, and Chase had just been leaving when he'd heard her muffled protests as a hand went somewhere she didn't want.

After that run-in, the guy didn't walk right for several weeks.

And the occurrence pretty much cemented a puppy love that just wouldn't die.

Everyone and their mother had known she had it bad for Chase throughout high school and the first two years of college. Christ, it was a well-known theory that wherever Mitch and Chase were, Madison wasn't too far behind. Sad as it was—and it *was* pathetic—she had attended the University of Maryland because they had.

Everything changed her junior year in college, the night he'd opened his first nightclub.

After that . . . she did everything in her power to avoid Chase. Not that it worked or anything.

One would think in a city as overpopulated as Washington, DC, she'd be able to avoid the rat bastard, but oh no, the laws of nature were a cruel, unrelenting bitch.

Chase was everywhere. She'd rented one of the smaller apartments on the second floor of the Gallery, and weeks later, he'd bought one of the penthouses on the top floor. Even on family holidays, he and his brothers had seats at her parents' dinner table, since they treated the Gambles like a flock of sons.

Working out at the gym, he'd be there pumping iron early in the morning while she did her daily pretend-run on the elliptical. And when he got on the treadmill? Oh, wow, who knew calf muscles could be so sexy? It wasn't her fault that she stared and maybe drooled on herself a little. Had *maybe* fallen off the elliptical a time or two when he'd lifted his shirt, revealing abs that looked like someone stuck paint rollers under his skin for crying out loud, and wiped his brow with the hem.

Who wouldn't be driven to distraction and take a tumble?

Hell, if Madison went to the local grocery on the corner, he'd be there, too, feeling up the peaches with his wonderfully long fingers—fingers that no doubt knew how to strum a guitar just as well as they knew how to work a woman into the height of sexual frenzy and then some.

Because she did know—oh, did she ever know how good he was.

Of course, half of DC probably knew how good he was with those hands of his by now.

5

"You have that look on your face." Bridget raised a brow at her. "I know that look."

Madison shook her head in denial. She really needed to stop thinking about his fingers, but there was no escaping her childhood crush—the embodiment of every fantasy she'd ever had. An infatuation she never grew out of and the reason why no other guy lasted longer than a few months, though she'd take that little ditty to the grave.

Chase was the Antichrist to her.

A really, unbelievably hot Antichrist . . .

Suddenly it was way too warm, and she tugged on the edge of her blouse and scowled at the invitation. It was only four days in the romantic, upscale vineyards. Hundreds of people would be there, and even though she had to deal with Chase during the rehearsal and wedding, she could easily find creative ways to avoid him.

But the nervous flutter in the pit of her stomach, the excitement that hummed in her veins, was telling a whole different story, because seriously, how was she going to steer clear of the only man she'd ever loved . . . *and* wanted to maim?

"Toss me that employee directory," Madison said, wondering if Derek might be available after all.

The drive to Hillsboro, Virginia, on Wednesday morning wasn't a pain, since everyone else was streaming into the city for his or her daily commute, but Madison was driving as though she was auditioning for NASCAR.

According to the three missed calls from her mother—who thought Madison had been kidnapped in the big, bad

city and was now being held for an ungodly sum of money—
the four text messages from her brother wondering if she
knew how to navigate the beltway—because apparently
little sisters couldn't drive—and the voice mail from her
father warning there was a problem with the reservations,
she was late for brunch.

Who in the hell still ate brunch?

Thrumming her fingers against the steering wheel, she
squinted as the late May sun glared off the exit sign. Yep—
as she zoomed on by—she'd missed the exit.

Damn it.

Tossing a glare at her cell phone, because she so knew it
was going to ring in a hot second, she darted into the other
lane and took the next exit so she could backtrack to where
she needed to be.

She wouldn't be running late and be so . . . so discom-
bobulated if she had spent last night packing like a normal,
emotionally stable woman in her mid-twenties—a successful, emotionally stable woman—instead of bemoaning the
fact she had to walk arm-in-arm down the aisle with Chase,
because, for real, that was just plain cruel. The fact that
Derek had another date that weekend and couldn't accom-
pany her was like adding insult to injury.

Her cell phone went off the moment the wheels on her
Charger hit the correct exit ramp and she growled at it, wish-
ing the damn thing into the tenth circle of hell. Were there ten
circles? Who knew, but she figured by the time everyone got
drinks in them and started talking about how Madison used
to run around shirtless as a child, there'd be twenty circles to
hell, and she'd have visited every one of them.

Tall black walnut trees crowded either side of the rural route she flew down, shading the road and giving it an almost ethereal feel. Up ahead, the deep blue of the mountains loomed over the valley. There was no doubt, as long as the weather held up, the outdoor wedding was going to be beautiful.

A sudden pop jerked her chin up and the steering wheel to the left, right, and then left again. Heart racing, she gripped the wheel as she weaved and crossed the centerline like a poster child for DUIs.

"Damn it," she muttered, eyes going wide as she regained control of the Charger. A tire had blown—a mother-freaking tire had blown. "Why not?"

Debating whether or not to attempt the next ten miles on her rim, she strung together an atrocity of curse words that would've made her brother blush. She whipped the wheel to the right and coasted to a stop on the shoulder of the road. Throwing the car into park, she debated getting out and kicking the damn car. Instead, she did the mature thing: placed her head on the steering wheel and cussed some more.

This was so not starting out well.

Lifting her head, her gaze slid to her cell phone. She snatched it off the seat, thumbed through her contacts, and quickly hit the call button. After only two rings, someone grabbed the line.

"Maddie? Where in the hell are you, girl?" Her father's concerned voice exploded. "Your mother's about to call the state police, and I'm not sure how much—"

"Dad, I'm fine. I blew a tire about ten miles out."

Over the sounds of laughter and clanking silverware, her father huffed. "You did what?"

Her stomach rumbled, reminding her that it was past eleven and she hadn't had breakfast yet. "I blew a tire."

"You blew what?"

Madison rolled her eyes. "I blew a tire."

"Wait. I can't hear you. Guys, can you keep it down?" His voice got a little farther away from the mouthpiece. "Maddie's on the phone and she blew something." The room erupted in male laughter.

Oh. My. Freaking. God.

"Sorry about that, honey. Now, what happened?" her father asked. "You blew a fire?"

"I blew a tire! A tire! You know those things that are round and made of rubber?"

"Oh. Oh! Now I get it." Dad chuckled. "It's an animal house in here, everyone eating all at once. Did you remember to get that spare tire of yours replaced since your last flat? You know, dear, you should always be prepared. What if you needed to leave town during an evacuation?"

She was seconds away from smacking her face off the steering wheel. She loved her parents to bits, but she really didn't want to talk about her lack of planning skills while a room full of men laughed about her blowing anything—while Chase laughed, because she'd definitely picked out his deep baritone in the background. Her belly was already filling with knots at the thought of seeing him soon. "I know, Dad, but I haven't had a chance to get a new spare tire yet."

"You should always have a spare. Have we not taught you anything about preparedness?"

Well, wasn't that a moot point right now? And it wasn't like a comet had struck her car.

Her father sighed like all fathers do when their daughters need rescuing, no matter how old they were. "Just sit tight, and we'll come get you, honey."

"Thanks, Dad." She ended the call and dropped the cell into her purse.

It was so easy imagining her absurdly large family crowded around the table, shaking their heads. Only Maddie would be late. Only Maddie would blow a tire and not have a spare. Being the youngest in a family that consisted of blood relations and the Gamble horde sucked.

No matter what she did, she was always little, itty bitty Maddie. Not Madison, who oversaw the volunteer services at the Smithsonian Library. Being a history geek growing up, she considered her career choice fitting.

Madison tipped her head back against the headrest and closed her eyes. Even with the air conditioner running, heat from the outside had begun to seep in. She undid the first couple of buttons and was grateful she'd opted for light-weight linen pants instead of jeans. Knowing her luck, she'd get heat stroke before her dad or brother showed up.

She hated knowing she was dragging either of them away from the start of the celebrations. That was the last thing she wanted. And right next to the last thing was the fact there was no doubt in her mind that Chase was probably shaking his head along with everyone else.

A few minutes passed and she must've dozed off because the next thing she knew, someone was tapping on her window.

Blinking slowly, she pressed the button to lower the

window and turned her head to stare into a pair of cerulean blue eyes fanned by incredibly thick black lashes.

Oh . . . oh, no . . .

Her heart stuttered and tumbled over itself as her gaze drifted across high cheekbones she was painfully familiar with, full lips that looked tantalizingly soft but could be firm and unyielding. Dark brown hair fell over his forehead, always a shy away from needing a haircut. A strong nose with a slight bump from a break during his college years gave the otherwise flawless male beauty a hard, dangerously sexy edge.

Madison's gaze dipped over the plain white shirt that clung to broad shoulders, a rock-hard chest, and a narrow waist. Jeans hung low on his hips and thank God the rest of the view was cut off by the car door.

Forcing her gaze back to his face, she sucked in a sharp breath.

Those lips had curved into a knowing half smile that did funny things to her insides. And like a match tossed to gasoline, her body sparked alive and flames licked every inch of her.

She loathed her immediate response to him, wished any other eligible guy in the tri-state area could evoke the same inferno, and yet was thrilled by it. Absolutely undone.

"Chase," she breathed.

His grin spread and damn, there were those dimples. "Maddie?"

Her body quivered at the sound of his voice. It was deep and smooth like aged whiskey. That voice should be outlawed, along with the rest of the package. Her gaze dropped again.

Damn the car door, because no doubt that package was quite impressive.

For a brief, unwanted second, she was thrown back to her junior year of college, to the night she had visited Chase's club for the very first time and stood in his posh office. Full of hope, full of wanting . . .

Snapping out of her stupor, she sat up, her spine rigid. "They sent *you*?"

He chuckled, as if she'd uttered the funniest thing in the world. "I volunteered, actually."

"You did?"

"Of course," he drawled lazily. "I had to come see what little Maddie Daniels was blowing."

Chapter Two

About a second after those words left his mouth, Chase realized his mistake, but damn, he didn't regret them. A fierce, hot, and downright sinful flush stole across her cheeks and down her throat. There was a part of him—a ruthless fragment—that would break legs and crush hands to see how far that blush traveled.

But like he'd learned before, at the last possible second, Maddie Daniels was a line not meant to be crossed.

Her pouty lips thinned and anger flared in her hazel eyes, turning them more green than brown. Her eyes shifted colors based on her emotions, and lately he'd seen them green more times than not.

"That was kind of crude, Chase."

He shrugged. Civility wasn't his middle name. "Are you going to stay in the car or get out?"

Maddie looked like she would have to be torn from the car. "Am I supposed to just leave it here, along the side of the road?"

"I called a tow truck, and they're on their way. If you pop your trunk, I'll get your stuff."

Her gaze finally moved past him, and he felt his chest ease. "Nice car," she said.

Chase looked over his shoulder at the black Porsche gleaming in the sunlight. "It's a car." One of three he owned. He wished he'd brought his truck instead, but the thing guzzled gas like nothing else. Turning back to the little problem at hand, he stepped aside. "Maddie, are you coming with me or not?"

She stared up at him, almost defiantly, which was laughable. Maddie was all of five foot three and probably weighed a buck ten. He towered over her and could easily throw her over his shoulder with one arm.

Their eyes locked.

With each passing second, pulling her out of the car and throwing her over his shoulder seemed more likely. Maybe he'd give her a spanking he damn well knew she deserved.

Cock said yes by swelling almost painfully in his jeans.

Common sense said no with the punch to the gut.

If Chase was anything in life, he was his father—successful at a young age, determined, wealthy, and carrying the family gene enabling him to fuck up any serious relationship within ten seconds.

And everyone, even Maddie, knew he was just like his father.

So it's definitely time for a better tactic, he thought, taking a deep breath. "There's a slice of cheesecake your mom put aside with your name on it."

Maddie's eyes glazed over. He'd seen that look a few times before. Chocolate and desserts had given her that post-sex-bliss look ever since he could remember, and that wasn't helping with the problem in his jeans.

The car door flew open without any warning, and he

narrowly avoided accidental impotency by jumping out of the way.

"Cheesecake," she repeated, grinning. "Does it have strawberry topping?"

He fought a grin. "With a side of chocolate for dipping, just like you love."

She popped her hands on her curvy hips and cocked her head to the side. "Then what are you waiting for?" She pushed a button on her keys, and the trunk popped open. "Every second that passes between me and that cheesecake, the more dangerous this trip will get."

This trip was already dangerous.

He stalked to the back of her truck while she grabbed items from the backseat. Only one suitcase rested in the trunk. Maddie was always a light packer. He'd dated girls who couldn't stay a night away without three outfits and a dozen pairs of shoes. Maddie was low maintenance, probably a product of growing up with a bunch of rowdy boys.

Grabbing her luggage, he slammed the trunk, then rounded the rear of her car and drew up short. Jesus Christ . . .

She was bent over, tugging a long garment bag from the backseat. The thin linen of her pants stretched over the round ass he knew she worked hard for. How many times had he watched her on the elliptical at the gym? Too many times to count.

He really needed to start working out at a different time.

But he couldn't peel his eyes off her for the life of him. Maddie may be tiny, but she rocked some hellish curves, and even though she wasn't the type of woman he usually went for, she was beautiful in her own way. Perky nose and plump lips, cheekbones covered with a speckling of freckles. Long hair, currently pulled up, normally reached the middle of her back.

The kind of hair—the kind of body—a man could easily get lost in. Aw, hell, it was more than that. Maddie would make some son of a bitch a happy man one day. She was and always had been the complete package: smart, funny, strong-willed, and kind.

And that ass . . .

Chase pivoted around, inhaling through his nose, half tempted to drop Maddie off, drive into town, and pick up the first chick who looked his way. Or grab Maddie's rear.

She brushed past him, casting a weird look over her shoulder. "Are you dazing out on me? Let me guess. Bambi or Susie kept you up late? I can never tell them apart."

"You're talking about the Banks twins?"

Maddie cocked her head to the side and waited.

"Their names are Lucy and Lake," he corrected.

She rolled her eyes. "Who names their kid Lake? Oh! If you have kids, you can call them River and Stream." Shaking her head, her eyes narrowed. A knowing look crossed her face. "So you're still dating them?"

Honestly, *dating* wasn't the term he'd use for the tall, lanky twins. "I'm not dating them at the same time, Maddie. Nor have I."

"That's not what I've heard."

"Then you've heard wrong." But that look of hers spread. Clamping his jaw shut, he followed her. No point in correcting her assumption because his reputation was probably right up there with his father's already.

Opening the back door, she frowned. "Haven't made it to your room yet?"

He placed her bag in the trunk alongside his own. "Haven't checked in. I'd only arrived about fifteen minutes before your rescue call went out."

She smoothed invisible wrinkles from her pants, chin tucked low. "I didn't need rescuing."

Chase arched a mocking brow. "That's not how it looks to me."

"Just because I blew—"

"Say that again."

Maddie lifted her eyes to his again, and he felt their soulful depths in his gut. She could always take his breath away with a single look. "Say what?"

"Blew."

She rolled her eyes. "That's real mature."

"Anyway, you blew a tire and I had to come out here and get you. How is that not me rescuing you?"

Huffing, she spun around and returned to her car. With her purse in hand, she stalked over to the passenger side of his Porsche.

He grinned. "You should always have—"

"I know. A spare," she said, cutting him off and sliding into the car.

Laughing under his breath, he climbed in and sent her a sidelong glance. She was staring out the tinted window; her hand clutched her cell phone like a lifeline. He casually adjusted himself and prayed he got himself in check before her family swamped them again.

The first five miles back to the vineyard where his buddy

was getting married were quiet, not terse, but definitely not the most comfortable of experiences.

He should just ignore it. "Why are you pouting?"

"I'm not pouting." She cut him a dark look.

"Could've fooled me, Maddie."

"Stop calling me that." She dug around in her bag and pulled out a pair of sunglasses. She slid them on and then turned to him. Cute. "I hate it when you call me that."

"Why?"

She said nothing.

He sighed and went with a safe topic. "Your brother is really happy."

Beside him, Maddie relaxed a fraction. "I know. I'm really happy for him. He deserves this, right? He's so nice that any other girl would take advantage of that."

"He does." Chase's gaze flickered off the road. She was staring at him still, and he hated that the sunglasses blocked her eyes. He had no idea what the little terror was thinking behind those dark shades. "Lissa's a good girl. She'll do right by Mitch."

Maddie sucked her lower lip in and then said, "Mitch will do right by her."

A small smile tugged at his lips. "That is true. Though, marrying? Never thought I'd see the day when he settled down."

"I really don't want to hear about his escapades." She ran a hand over her hair, smoothing the few loose strands that had escaped her chignon. "I haven't eaten yet."

"Would a full stomach be better?"

She snorted.

"Remember that girl he was dating his sophomore year in college?"

Her eyes went wide, and his grin spread. "Oh, God—the one who actually started naming their kids on the first date?" she said, laughing. "What was her name?"

"Linda Bullock."

"Yes!" She popped up in her seat. "She had Mitch scared to death, calling him at all hours of the night. He got so mad when you told me about her."

"She camped outside our dorm after one date." Chase shook his head. "Pretty girl, but man, she was crazy."

They were coming up on the vineyards quickly. Before he knew it, Maddie would be surrounded by those who loved and cared for her, and he'd be back with his brothers, watching them troll the guest list for the ladies.

As if she were reading his thoughts, she glanced at him. "I bet you and your brothers couldn't be happier."

"Why is that?"

Her lips formed a tight smile. "It's a wedding, which means easy pickings."

"Are you saying I need easy pickings?"

"Maybe."

He chuckled and said, "I think you know better than that."

A red blush stained her cheeks under the sunglasses. Seeing her face flame attractively was almost worth going there with her, rehashing memories that needed to stay memories.

"Okay," she said. "You don't need easy pickings. I'm not saying that."

"Then what are you saying, Maddie?"

Frustration rolled off her as she ran her hand across the buttery leather of the car seats in long, languid strokes that made his dick twitch. "Lissa has a lot of pretty friends. Not the Banks twins, but still."

Chase nodded and then reached up for the sun visor, pulling out his own sunglasses. "She does."

"So, like I said, you and your brothers are going to have fun."

"Maybe." He reached across the seat, tapping his fingers off her forearm to get her attention and point out the long rows of grape vines slicing through the valley on his left. Immediately, she jerked back, and he raised his brows, kind of offended. "Touchy?"

"No. Sorry. Too much caffeine."

Then it struck him. Sometimes Chase forgot that their relationship wasn't like it used to be, and damn if that didn't suck.

She cleared her throat. "So, when are you guys going to get married?"

Chase barked with stilted laughter. "Good God, Maddie."

"What?" Her frown pulled the corners of her lips down. "It's not an insane question. You all are getting up there in age."

Shaking his head, he laughed again. He was twenty-eight, not an old man. Chad, his middle brother, was thirty, and his oldest brother, Chandler, was thirty-one. None of them approached marriage with open arms. Not after seeing what it did to their parents. Or, in reality, what his father did to his mother. It was why the three of them had practically grown up in the Daniels' household.

Maddie leaned across the seat, punching him in the thigh with a little fist. "Stop laughing at me, jerk."

"I can't help it. You're funny."

"Whatever."

Grinning, he took the next left to the private road leading up to the vineyard. "I don't know about marriage, Maddie. You know what they say about us."

"Who's going to take a risk on the Gamble boys? Or take a 'gamble' on the Gamble boys." She gave a small shake of her head. "We aren't in high school or college anymore, Chase."

His gaze drifted from the sleek line of her thigh, up to where the buttons of her blouse parted, revealing a tantalizing swell of breast.

"Yeah," he said, focusing on the road. His knuckles ached from how tightly he was gripping the stick shift. "We're definitely not in school anymore."

There was a quick grin before she turned back to her window, appearing to soak in the rolling hills, but then she had to go there. "You're not like your father, Chase."

"You of all people should know that I'm exactly like my father," he snapped back, voice harder than he'd intended.

Maddie's gaze swung back to him, her cheeks paling and then flushing. Her mouth opened, but she clamped it shut and turned back to the window.

He groaned. "Shit, Maddie, I didn't mean it like—"

"It's fine. Whatever."

Fine and *whatever* were words he knew were code for *pissed off*. They were the same words his mother had used time and time again when his father didn't come home at night or disappeared on an unexpected business trip.

Chase cursed again.

Driving up the winding road, he fought the urge to apologize. It was better this way. For several years, Maddie had been nothing more than Mitch's kid sister. Yeah, he was protective of her, but that was a given. That one night, so many years ago, had mucked up things between them forever. And if Chase knew anything, he knew there were no do-overs.

Just like there had been no do-overs for his parents.

On the way into the main lodge, Madison did her best not to stare at Chase, not to get drawn into that swagger of his, fall into the web he had no idea he was weaving just by being next to her. So she stared straight ahead and ignored him.

An elderly couple inched their way down the pathway, their hands joined together tightly. The looks they shared were so full of love that Madison felt a pang of envy. That was the kind of love she had dreamed of as a little girl—love that didn't dull after the decades but only grew stronger.

The woman's thick-soled shoes slipped on one of the pebbles. Her husband easily caught her arm, but her purse dropped off her other arm, spilling the contents along the white stones.

Madison rushed forward, kneeling down as she quickly scooped up the lady's belongings.

"Oh, thank you, dear," the old woman crooned. "I'm getting terribly clumsily in my old age."

"It's no problem." Madison smiled, handing the purse back. "Have a nice day."

Returning to Chase's side, she found him smiling at her. Not a full smile that showed off those dimples, but a small, private one. "What?"

"Nothing," he said with a slight shake of his head.

The moment Madison stepped inside the cozy atrium of Belle's Vineyard, her family attacked her. Bone-breaking hugs were given by first cousins, second cousins, a few people she didn't even recognize, and an uncle. Hugs that lifted her clear off her feet and left her a little dizzy.

But when she saw her brother beyond the atrium, standing before several long tables covered in white linen, a wide smile broke out across her face and she took off.

Mitch was tall, like their father, and his brown hair was clipped close to his skull. With his all-American good looks and sweet disposition, he usually had a legion of women swooning at his feet. Many of them included her friends. The single ones were no doubt mourning this weekend, but he'd only ever had eyes for Lissa.

He caught her halfway and spun her around. "We were starting to think you were boycotting the wedding."

"Never!" She laughed, clasping his arms. Not since Christmas had she gotten to see her brother. He and Lissa had moved to nearby Fairfax and with their busy careers, it left little time for family reunions. "I've missed you."

"Now come on, don't start crying on me already."

She blinked. "I'm not crying."

"Good." He enveloped her in another massive hug. "I think you may've grown about two inches."

Laughing, she wiggled free. "I stopped growing, like, ten years ago."

"Try twenty years ago." Her father's booming voice carried from the head of the table. This bear of a man was probably aghast that one of his offspring could've auditioned for the Lollipop Guild.

Over Mitch's shoulder, Lissa waited with a welcoming smile. Pulling free of her brother, Madison approached the slender blonde and gave her a tight hug.

"I'm so happy you're here," Lissa said, pulling back. Tears filled her gray eyes. "Everything is perfect now. Come, your mom is saving you dessert."

Trailing after her, Madison glanced over her shoulder. Mitch had his hand on Chase's shoulder and they both were laughing. A heartbeat passed, and Chase looked up, his eyes meeting hers.

Madison looked away and nearly ran straight into Chandler. Bigger and brawnier than all the Gamble brothers, he was easily the most intimidating. All three brothers shared the same strong features and extraordinary blue eyes, but Chandler was taller than the other two by a good three inches.

"Careful, squirt," he said, easing past her. "Don't want to run over one of the bridesmaids."

Squirt? "Thanks, Godzilla."

Then he had the gall to ruffle her hair like she was twelve.

She swung on him, missing by a mile, which was impressive considering how bulky he was.

Chandler laughed as he joined Mitch and his brother. So far, she hadn't spied the middle brother. Chad was a notorious prankster and no one was safe when he was around.

Megan Daniels sat beside Madison's father in the large, domed room, and it was hard to believe that her mom was approaching her fifty-sixth birthday. There wasn't a single gray hair in the mass of her auburn waves.

"Sit, honey." She patted the seat next to her. "I saved you some cheesecake."

Without being told twice, Madison took her place and dug in, listening to the flow of conversation around her as everyone else settled back around the long tables. Every once in a while, a cousin twice removed would appear and then some of Lissa's family. Her parents seemed nice and got along with Madison's.

Mr. Grant, Lissa's father, even smiled when Madison's dad launched into the next wave of generators that could keep a 1,200-square-foot bunker running.

Her mother rolled her eyes. "You know your father likes to talk shop."

Yeah, but most people's shoptalk didn't revolve around an apocalypse.

With everyone occupied, she swiped the last two cookies off a platter and practically swallowed them whole. If this was considered "brunch," Madison thought she might just have a new favorite meal.

"It was really nice of Chase to volunteer to pick you up, honey." Her mom's eyes twinkled. "He wasn't even here for ten minutes, but he left right away to get you."

Madison almost choked on the cookie. "Yeah, really nice of him."

Her mom leaned in and lowered her voice. "You know, he's still single."

Clearing her throat, she was thankful Chase was nowhere near the table. "Good for him."

25

"And you used to have the biggest crush on him. It was so cute."

Madison's mouth dropped open to deny it, but Mrs. Grant responded before she could say a word. "A crush on who?"

"Chase." Her mother nodded sagely toward the front of the room. "She followed Mitch and him around like a—"

"Mom," Madison groaned, wanting to hide under the table. "I did not follow them around like a puppy."

Her mother just smiled.

"That is so sweet," Mrs. Grant said, her gaze traveling up to where Chase and the rest of the men stood. "And he seems like a lovely young man. Mitch was telling us how he owns several nightclubs in the city."

Mom launched into a detailed account of Chase's successes, which were quite impressive. Within the last seven years, he'd started several profitable upscale bars, easily placing him as one of the most eligible bachelors in the District.

But her mother had glossed over Chase's well-known playboy social life. Madison hadn't been to any of his clubs since she was twenty-one, since that disastrous night when alcohol and several years of crushing on a guy came to an utterly humiliating head.

After taking a sip of water, she excused herself to check on her room reservation and strolled between the tables and out into the wide foyer on her way to the reservation desk. Once outside the breakfast area though, she realized she had company.

Chase fell into step beside her, hands shoved into the

pockets of his jeans. He was a good head and then some taller than her, and she always felt like a dwarf standing next to him.

She arched a brow at him, totally trying to play it cool even though her heart was pounding walking this close to him. "Following me?"

"Thought I'd change up the pattern."

"Ha. Ha."

He flashed a grin. "Actually, I was going to pick up my cabin key."

"So am I." Belle Vineyards had several cabins nestled across their estate, and they had reserved most of them for those attending the wedding scheduled for Saturday. She bit her lip, realizing she hadn't thanked him yet. "Thank you for coming and getting me. You didn't have to."

Chase shrugged but said nothing. They wound their way through the elegantly designed hallways with exposed log walls and eventually arrived at the front desk.

An older man behind the counter with a nametag reading BOB smiled at them. "How can I help you?"

Chase leaned against the desk. "We're here to pick up our room keys."

"Oh, for the wedding?" His hands paused over the keyboard, ready to fly. "Congratulations."

Madison choked back a laugh. "We aren't. I mean, there's no need for congratulations. He and I aren't like that. We aren't—"

"What she's trying to say is that we're not the bride and groom," Chase replied evenly, smirking. God forbid anyone thought that. Geez. "We're with the bridal party."

Chase gave their names while Madison mentally kicked herself for sputtering like an inept teenager, but standing this close to him was more than distracting. His presence, his spicy scent that was part cologne and part male, had her senses firing left and right.

He always had to stand close. Like right now, there was barely an inch between their bodies. She could feel the natural heat that rolled off him and if she closed her eyes, she was pretty sure she could remember what it felt like to have his arm around her, cradling her to his hard chest as his hand skated under the hem of the dress she'd worn just for him, sliding up . . .

Madison pulled herself from the memory. So not going there.

"I'm sorry," the clerk said, drawing her attention back to what was important. "There's been an unfortunate mix-up."

Suddenly, she remembered her father's message. "Has something happened?"

The clerk's cheeks turned ruddy. "We had another wedding party that ends on Friday, and, well, to put this bluntly, one of the part-time workers overbooked the cabins, which pushed out the last two reservations made."

Which, of course, would've been Chase's and Madison's reservations, because if they had anything in common, they always did things last minute.

Chase frowned as he leaned a lot farther in. "Well, there's got to be a fix."

Swallowing visibly, he glanced at the computer. "I was under the impression that a Mrs. Daniels had already addressed this issue."

Madison had a really bad feeling.

"We explained the problem upon her arrival. We only have one cabin available, the old honeymoon suite about to be remodeled."

"Honeymoon suite?" Chase repeated slowly, as if those two words made no sense.

Her stomach dropped.

The clerk looked visibly uncomfortable. "Two people can definitely room there. Mrs. Daniels said it wouldn't be a problem."

She was going to kill her mother.

"I'm sorry." Chase drew up straight, and at over six feet tall, that was a lot of looking up to do. His voice was firm. "*We* cannot share a cabin."

Ouch. Sharing a room with Chase wasn't on her list of things to do, but damn, she wasn't the worse possible option.

"Money is not an issue," he continued, eyes darkening to a navy blue—a sure sign his temper was about to make an appearance. "I can pay double or triple to get two rooms."

Okay, now that was just insulting. She glared at him. "I agree. There's no way I can stay with *him*."

Chase cut her a look.

The clerk shook his head. "I'm sorry, but there are no other rooms available. It's the old honeymoon cabin . . . or it's nothing."

Both of them stared at the clerk. Madison had a sinking suspicion Chase was about to grab the man, turn him upside down, and shake him until room keys fell out. She could get behind that.

"Rooms should become available Friday morning, and

we will ensure both of you are first in line, but unfortunately, there isn't anything I can do."

Madison ran a hand over her hair, stunned. Rooming with Chase? There was no way. Between gawking at him in close proximity and wanting to beat him over the head when he opened his mouth, she was going to go insane.

The days leading up to the wedding were supposed to be fun and relaxing. Not a trip into crazy land. And her mom—her nutso, matchmaking mom—had a hand in this. She was going to bury that woman in a bomb shelter.

Madison peeked at the still-silent form of Chase. A muscle worked in his jaw like he was grinding his molars down to the gum. This was horrific for her, but for him? God, he was probably ready to make a bid for the clerk's room. No doubt this would put a major crimp in his woman-seducing plans.

"You have got to be kidding me." Chase twisted away, placing his hands on narrow hips. He swore under his breath. "All right, give me the damn keys."

Madison flushed. "Look, I can—"

"You can what? Room with your mom, who's on a second honeymoon with your dad? Or maybe you'd prefer to room with one of the other couples and ruin their romantic weekend?" A note attached to two keys dropped into his open palm. "Sleep in your car, even? We don't have a choice." His eyes met her wide ones. "We're stuck with each other until Friday."

Chapter Three

"Oh, man, you two are *not* going to make it to the wedding." Mitch leaned back in his chair, eyes glittering with amusement. "No way."

Madison sighed.

"Why?" her mother asked from the end of the table. "They'll do just fine."

"They'll kill each other," Mitch said with a laugh, and then he sobered. "They might actually kill each other."

Turning her eyes to the glass ceiling, Madison struggled for patience. "We aren't going to kill each other."

"I wouldn't make that promise," Chase muttered, speaking for the first time since they'd left the front desk.

God, she was two seconds from jumping on his back like a monkey and strangling him. But then he strode off, glancing over his shoulder at her.

"This train is leaving for the cabin now if you want a ride."

Trailing after him, she muttered, "Who hasn't had a ride?"

Chase stopped dead in his tracks. "Excuse me?"

"I said"—she gave him a saucy smirk—"who hasn't had a ride?"

He leveled her with a pointed look. "I can think of a few people."

Wow. He went there. She refused to allow herself to blush again. "Bet you could count them on one hand, too."

"Possibly," he murmured and started walking again.

The trip to the cabin—all the way toward the edge of the property, near the thick walnut trees at the mouth of the Blue Ridge Mountains—was silent and awkward.

The moment she'd made the crack about his sex life, she'd regretted it. Saying things like that only reinforced his misguided belief that he was just like his father. It was the thing she never got about him. She knew deep down that becoming like his unfaithful father was Chase's own personal nightmare, but he did nothing but barrel down that path with a different girl every week. She skirted around a thorny rose bush leaning into the path.

He'd been that way since high school—maybe not as bad as Chad, but Chase exemplified the playboy lifestyle.

And the fact that Chase was an equal opportunity bed jumper always stung, because he was open for business for everyone . . . everyone but her.

Outside the cabin, Chase held the key like it was a snake about to sink its fangs into his hand.

He hadn't said a word on the way down. He was pissed; she knew it. What red-blooded single male came to a wedding and enjoyed getting stuck with his best friend's little sister as his roommate? In an old honeymoon cabin on top of that?

Madison couldn't believe it. She literally had the worst luck when it came to him.

She checked her cell phone and wanted to throw it. No service.

Finally, he opened the door and reached along the wall, flipping on the light. Her jaw dropped, and she slapped a hand over her mouth.

This was a joke. It had to be. "Your brother has to be behind this," she said.

Chase shook his head slowly. "If he is, I'm going to kill him."

It was no wonder the clerk had said the room was scheduled for renovation. Clearly, someone had done a rush job cleaning the room. There was a faint smell of Lysol and potpourri that lingered in the spacy cabin, but the carpet . . . the bed.

Several throw rugs covered the wood flooring. They were every color of the rainbow, but one was a bear rug. An actual bear rug. The walls were painted a vibrant purple and red, and the bed . . . the bed was draped in red velvet and heart-shaped.

Chase strolled into the room, dropping his keys on a white dresser that looked like something her grandmother would have in her house. He glanced over his shoulder, one brow arched.

Madison busted into laughter. She couldn't help it. "It's like a seventies love shack."

A slow smile stretched across his lips. "I think I've seen this room in old-school porn videos."

She giggled as she followed him in. A quick peek in the bathroom revealed a tub the size of a pool, perfect for the frisky newlywed couple.

Looking over her shoulder, Chase shook his head. "You could fit five people in that thing."

"That might get awkward."

"Ah, true, but it's definitely big enough for two."

"I don't know," she said, turning away from the bathroom and strolling past him. Across from the bed were balcony doors that led to a deck and a Jacuzzi. "I never got the whole bathtub-sex thing."

"Then you've been doing it wrong." His breath was warm against her cheek, and dear God, wouldn't he know?

Startled by how quietly he had crept up on her, she spun around and swallowed. Images of him wet, naked, and wrapped around her in that bathtub sent a wave of molten lava shooting through her veins and straight to her core.

Her knees went weak. "I'm not doing anything wrong."

"Of course not," he drawled. "You've just had the wrong partner."

Madison wasn't a prude, and just because no man had ever lived up to Chase in her eyes didn't mean she hadn't dated. And maybe he was right and she just had the wrong partners, because she couldn't imagine not enjoying some bath time with him, but no way in hell would she ever admit as much to him.

Which meant it was time to change the subject and fast. But when she lifted her lashes and found him still staring at her beneath hooded eyes, her breath hitched in her throat.

Standing this close to him, inches away from a bed that would've made Austin Powers proud, was too much. The night in his club resurfaced in a rush of slippery emotions and tangled hopes that never really came to fruition.

She finally found her voice. "It . . . has nothing to do with my partners."

Chase cocked his head to the side, his intense blue eyes narrowing. "Partners as in plural?"

Feigning indifference, she rolled her eyes when her heart was racing. "I'm twenty-five, not sixteen."

"You don't have to remind me of how old you are," he all but growled.

"Then why do you seem shocked by the fact that I've had sex?"

He took a step forward, and she took one back. "With more than one person?"

Surely this wasn't breaking news. "How many people have you had sex with? Five hundred?" she threw back. "Hell, how many in one month?"

A clear warning formed in those sapphire-gem eyes. "We're not talking about me."

"And we're not talking about me." One more step and her back hit the wall. There was nowhere to go. "So, let's just stop . . ."

"Stop what?" He leaned in, his breath tantalizingly warm against her cheek, and he planted his large hands against the wall on either side of her head.

Madison's gaze dropped to his lips, and she hadn't the foggiest idea what they'd been talking about. Something about sex, and God, talking about sex with Chase was not a good idea. Because now she wanted sex. With Chase. She wanted to feel him inside her, only him, always him.

She wanted so much.

A liquid fire had spread through her veins, licking at her.

Lust rose so quickly, pulsing through her limbs, hitting her fast and hard, leaving her senses spinning. A small part of her brain that still functioned fired off warnings left and right. It was insanity to even entertain the idea of anything going down between her and Chase, but as her gaze moved up, colliding with his, her heart stopped.

"Tell me," he ordered, voice low and gravely. "How many boys have you let touch you?"

Part of her bristled at his demand, but the other incredibly stupid part was thrilled that he cared. "I've never been with *boys*, Chase."

Anger and something far more potent flared in his blue eyes. "Oh, so that's how it is."

"Whatever it is, it's none of your business."

He chuckled deeply. The movement brought his lips close to her cheek. "It's my business."

"Explain that faulty logic to me," she said.

Chase smiled. "You're my best friend's little sister. That makes it my business—all my business."

And that was the wrong thing to say. Fire of a different kind now pulsed through her. "Get away." She started to push off the wall, but Chase leaned in, his chest flush with hers. Her body went haywire. Anger. Lust. Hope. Love. Fear. All her emotions tangled together. "Chase . . ."

He said nothing, and all she could now concentrate on was the feel of his rock-hard chest pressed against her breasts. The thin cotton of his shirt and her blouse were no match for the heat that rolled off him or the heat building inside her. Her nipples hardened to aching, wanton pearls, and she dragged in a deep breath, biting back a moan.

His lips parted.

There was no hiding her reaction, not i
Chase who knew every flavor of woman. And sh
be his flavor—his favorite. A tight coil wound deep i

She was panting now, and he hadn't even really tou
her. She tried to disconnect from her out-of-contro
hormones, going as far as thinking about the DC Metro,
and still, her body was turning on her.

His breath hitched and then he scowled at her, even as
he pressed his forehead against hers. Her lashes fluttered
shut and she grew very still, barely daring to breathe as his
breath danced over her brow, down her temple, and across
her cheeks.

His lips hovered over hers.

"No," he snarled.

Madison wasn't sure to whom he was talking, but then
his mouth was crushing hers, and her world became him—
the touch and feel of his lips pressing down, forcing hers
to respond. It wasn't a gentle kiss or a sweet exploration. It
was angry and raw, breathtaking and soul burning. Right
now, she didn't want gentle. She wanted hard and fast,
him and her, on the floor, even the bear rug, both of them
naked and sweating.

His tongue was a moist, hot demand inside her mouth,
parrying with hers until he took complete control and
flicked the tip of his tongue over the roof of her mouth.
There was a delicious possessiveness in the way he kissed
her, as if he were staking his claim at the same time he was
burning away the memories of anyone else for her. And he
did. In an instant, there was nobody but him.

and his palm splayed flat
the arch of her neck. He
odds with the fierceness of
ays wanted Chase, how she
and how she had once had
e moaned, melting into him.
d for him. Her body—
r eyes snapped open, her chest
le stared at her . . . stared at her
like she had ... g terribly wrong. And he . . . *he*
had kissed *her*.

Walking backward, Chase shook his head, his hands
clenching at his sides. "That . . . that didn't happen."

She blinked over the wrenching pull in her chest. "But . . .
it did."

His striking face went impassively indifferent, and it felt
like Madison had been punched in the gut. "No. No," he
said. "It didn't."

And with that, he spun around and stormed out of the
cabin, slamming the door behind him.

Madison blinked slowly. Oh, hell to the no, he did not just
storm out of there like a drama queen. She was going to find
him and then castrate him.

She winced.

Okay, maybe not that extreme, but she'd be damned if
she let him kiss her like that and then run.

Madison was well on her way to getting drunk.

Not fall-on-your-face or strip-off-your-clothes drunk,
although without all the family around that might have

38

sounded fun, but there was definitely a wine-induced headache in her near future.

Sitting on a bench along the sprawling deck outside the main lodge, she inhaled the scent of mountain air and grapes. Members of her family and Lissa's chattered around her. The low hum of conversation would've normally been soothing as she was a lover of all sorts of background noise, but right now, she wanted to slide through the narrow spaces in the wooden rail around the deck and fade into the night. Taking another long sip, she gazed out over the lawn. Paper lanterns hung from the poles spaced along the pebbled pathway, casting a faint light across the grounds.

She glanced down at her third glass of Petit and bit back a strangled giggle. Such a lightweight, but the heady thrum in her veins helped ease the mixture of shame and unquenched lust that burned in her stomach. An all-too-familiar feeling after a rather idiotic run-in with Chase.

He had kissed her.

And then, in the ultimate heart crusher, he'd wanted her to forget it. Been there, done that, and she definitely had the wounded heart to prove it.

Why had he kissed her if he was so obviously disgusted by the idea? Who knew. Maybe the answer was in the depths of her dark purplish wine?

Her father's boisterous laughter brought a faint smile to her face, and she twisted around on the bench. He stood with her brother and two of the three Gamble men. Chase was hiding somewhere else, most likely from her.

After he'd kissed her—and she felt the need to keep reminding herself that it had been he who'd kissed her—she hadn't seen him. Like the child he treated her as, she'd conveniently hid away in the bathroom while he deposited their luggage in the gaudiest cabin ever. Not her proudest moment.

Madison just couldn't make sense of any of it, and it wasn't fair. The last thing she wanted to be dealing with during her brother's wedding was this. It was a time to celebrate and laugh, not a time to add another notch on the humiliation belt.

But of course, here she was, grateful that it was dark enough to hide the flush that hadn't faded yet. Worse still, that kiss had sent her spiraling backward in time to the one night she never wanted to remember but also didn't want to forget. Except now she couldn't stop the onslaught of little vignettes replaying from that evening.

It had been her junior year in college, and as usual, she was in between boyfriends, still madly infatuated with her childhood crush, and the happy owner of one sexy little black dress that months of her part-time research gig at the university had paid for.

The opening night of Chase's nightclub, Komodo, had changed everything. All these years and it seemed like yesterday. The drinks. The dancing. Everyone had been there—her brother, Lissa, Chase's brothers, her friends. It had been a great night, one for celebrating. The evening had been a raving success, and Madison had been unbelievably proud. So many people had doubted him, but she never had.

It had been past closing time. Her brother and most of her friends had already gone home when she found Chase in his penthouse office on the third floor, staring at the landscape of the city. The straight line of his spine, the perfectly tailored cut of his suit across his broad shoulders had stolen her breath. She'd stood there for what seemed like hours but was probably the barest of seconds before Chase had turned to her and smiled . . . smiled just for her.

Madison had ventured into his office, complimented him eagerly on the success of the club, and listened to his plans to open two more: one in Bethesda and another in Baltimore. She'd felt special that he had included her in such knowledge. It was like she belonged next to him for the first time and that thrilled her.

Both of them had been drinking, but neither of them had been three sheets to the wind. Alcohol may've been the proverbial courage in the bottle, but it couldn't be blamed for what happened next.

She'd moved toward him, only to give him a hug goodbye, but when his arms had returned the gesture and she'd tipped her head back, something amazing and crazy happened.

Chase had kissed her—gently, carefully, and so sweetly that in a heady heartbeat, she had really thought all of her dreams had been coming true. Before she'd known it, he'd settled onto one of the supple leather couches in his office, pulled her onto his lap, and the kisses . . . Oh, God, the kisses then had been blatantly carnal and claiming, erotically promising. His fingers were quick and deft, moving the zipper of her dress down, revealing her to his heated stare. His hands had been everywhere, skimming over her breasts, sneaking under the dress, discovering for the first time one of Madison's oddities: She hated wearing panties. And he had gone crazy then, easing her onto her back, his fingers finding her most hidden places and thrusting as his body and tongue mimicked the movements.

When she had cried out his name, he'd gone incredibly still, his breathing ragged a second before he tore himself away from her and ended up pacing clear across the room like a jungle cat.

There hadn't been much time for her to be confused. Chase had freaked, ushering her out of his office, and the very next day, he'd called her, apologized for his drunken behavior, and promised that it would never happen again.

And it hadn't . . . until several hours ago.

At least now, he couldn't blame alcohol. He had no excuse, but he had broken her heart back then, shattered it into a million useless little pieces. As sad as it was, she hadn't fully recovered from his obvious regret. It stung, left an aching pierce that hit her in the chest when she least expected it.

Obviously, he hadn't been as attracted to her as she to him. Sure, there had to have been something there between the two of them, but it was unequal. She wanted more. And he had wanted just a taste, got it, and decided he didn't want any more, which was usually his MO. And earlier today? Perhaps he'd just been bored. Or maybe he wanted to see if she still wanted him and when he did, he'd discarded her like he had that night.

Madison sucked in a sharp breath. He wasn't a bad guy, though; she knew that. He just wasn't the guy for her.

Stupid tears burned her eyes, and she blinked them away.

Crying over Chase had been an almost nightly occurrence in college, especially when he began dating every woman in the city after the night at his club and the subsequent apology. So many girls that she never bothered to keep them straight. Didn't help they all looked alike: insanely tall, long-legged, blond, and big chested.

The exact opposite of Madison.

Snorting, she took another drink of her wine. Served her right, she supposed. Chase was and always would be a no-Madison-land. The kiss had been a fluke, a breach in sanity.

"Madison?" Lissa's soft voice interrupted her thoughts.

She looked up and smiled. "Hey there."

"You're awfully quiet tonight." The bride-to-be sat down beside her, glowing in her white sundress. "Are you worried about your car? Mitch said the tow truck brought it by a few hours ago."

"Oh, no, the car is fine. Dad is going to get a tire for me tomorrow. I'm . . . I'm just letting it all soak in." Madison's gaze flitted over the guests. "It's really beautiful here."

"Isn't it?" Lissa sighed. "Mitch and I visited two summers ago, during one of the festivals that offered a hot air balloon ride. With the aerial view, we sort of fell in love with the place."

"I can see the appeal." Though Madison was much more likely to be married with a baby on the way this time next year than her rosy-red ass getting into a hot air balloon. "You must be so excited."

"I am!" Her smile increased in wattage, and Madison couldn't help but return the expression over the rim of her wineglass. Lissa's smiles were always infectious. "Your brother is a wonderful man, and I couldn't be happier or luckier."

"I'm sure he's thinking the same thing."

Her eyes misted over. "Yes, I believe so. That's sort of perfect, isn't it?"

A lump suddenly formed in Madison's throat, so she washed it down with the rest of her wine. "Yes."

Lissa's gaze slid to her. "You look really nice tonight."

"Really?" She plucked at the sleeveless, gauzy blue dress that ended just below her thighs. It was a dark cobalt blue, but it had nothing on . . . She shook her head. So not going there. "Thank you."

A loud manly roar rose from where her father stood. Madison turned and her breath got stuck in her throat. Chase had arrived.

Madison glanced down at her empty glass and groaned under her breath.

Lissa nudged her. "He's something else, isn't he?"

She raised an eyebrow and muttered, "Something, all right."

Mistaking her comment as pleasant, Lissa went on. "Mitch told me how the three of you were the closest out of the Gamble brothers. I can't believe any of them are single. Each of them is so successful and handsome." Her smile turned sly. "Your mother said you had a crush on Chase growing up."

"Did she?" Madison desperately started searching for the waiter she'd seen earlier carrying a tray full of wineglasses.

Lissa nodded. "As soon as he heard your car was broken

down, he raced off to rescue you." She giggled, and Madison wanted to punch something. "He hadn't even been here for five minutes. It was all very sweet."

Like before, she refused to read too much into his motivations. Then she spied the crisp white shirt of the server. *Bingo!*

"Have you ever considered . . . ?"

Madison turned hot and then cold. "Considered what?"

"You know, being more than friends with Chase? I know you two have known each other since forever, but some of the best loves are those that start as friends. Take Mitch and me, for example. We were friends in the beginning."

Oh, sweet baby Jesus. Madison started waving her arm at the waiter like a madwoman.

"Thirsty?" Lissa asked, grinning.

"Very." She snatched a glass off the tray with a quick thank-you and a smile, and then considered grabbing two if this conversation was heading where it seemed to be.

Lissa's eyes twinkled. "And since you two are staying together here, there'll never be a better time to explore other possibilities than in such a romantic place."

Aw, what the hell. Madison grabbed another glass before the waiter escaped. She was going to need it.

Chapter Four

Chase was having one hell of a time listening to what his brothers and Mitch were talking about. Something about the wedding night and performance anxiety. What the hell did his brothers know about the first night as husband and wife? They had just as much experience as Mitch did.

His middle brother, Chad, had finally shown up and after Mitch's father had gone to claim his woman for the evening, he started giving pointers.

"Did you shave your boys?" Chad asked, holding a can of beer while everyone else had wine.

"What?" Mitch laughed.

"Shave the boys." Chad grinned. "The ladies love it when they're all smooth."

There was no doubt in his mind that Chad knew exactly what the ladies loved. Everyone in DC believed Chase was the man-whore of the clan, but in reality, it was Chad.

"I really don't want to talk about my balls with you," Mitch said. "Not now. Not ever."

Chase snickered. "Thank God."

"You'll be sorry if you don't." Chad smiled that

shit-eating grin of his. "You should also bring in some toys. That will . . ."

Chase zoned his brother out at that point. He wouldn't be surprised if Chad already had Mitch's honeymoon cabin decked out with all kinds of perverse things just for the fun of it.

Leaning against the railing, Chase took in the group around him. Most had already left, including Mitch's and Lissa's parents. The younger crowd was still up, though— the type of people who'd be at one of his clubs.

His skin itched. He hated being away for days without the ability to make sure things were running smoothly. His managers were on the up and up, more than able to keep the wheels churning, but even though it would be a slow night, he was having a hell of a time fighting the urge to call and check in every five seconds.

He was also having a hell of a time not thinking about what went down in that God-awful cabin. Fuck. What in the hell had he been thinking? Kissing Maddie—again? He glanced at Mitch and could almost feel his balls being castrated. And he'd deserve it. With his reputation, Chase was sure that Mitch wouldn't be too pleased to know Chase had molested his sister. Though Mitch had never outright condemned the idea—hell, several times he'd actually suggested Chase and Maddie get together—there was no way that was going to happen. And he doubted Mitch would be so supportive if it became reality and one took into consideration Chase's track record with women and the DNA he shared with his father. Mitch's suggestions weren't a green light.

Folding his arms, he ran his gaze over the sea of faces laughing and drinking around him.

There she was, by the benches. She had to be on her fourth glass of wine by now due to the amount of empty ones sitting around her, and if she was still anything like he remembered, this was going to be a long, albeit interesting, night.

Maddie.

Little freaking Maddie . . .

When he'd kissed her earlier . . . God, he didn't know a more responsive woman. The way she arched into him . . . The breathy feminine sound she made had nearly undone him, and that had been his wake-up call, but she had been so damn hot.

She was still too damn hot.

Chase widened his stance, biting back a growl. What had happened this afternoon, like what had happened that night in his club, had been a mistake. A mistake he enjoyed, but something that couldn't happen again. That was his best friend's sister . . .

Who was now standing on a bench, a half-empty wineglass hanging from her slender fingers as she swayed her hips to the light thrum of music coming from inside.

God. Damn.

One of Mitch's work buddies stood below her, grinning like he just won the fucking lottery or something. Or, as she raised her arms and her body moved in sensual curves to the rhythm of the music, the guy was thinking his chances of getting laid tonight were pretty high.

Without thinking, Chase pushed off the railing and took a

step toward them. Seconds away from walking right up to her and pulling her off that damn bench, he forced himself to stop. What the hell was he doing? She wasn't his problem.

But damn if a part of him wanted her to be his problem.

Going back to leaning on the railing, he clenched his jaw shut so tightly that his teeth ached. Who was that tool talking to her, coaxing her off the bench? Robby? Bobby? Some dickhead name like that?

Whoever he was, he reached up, placed his hands on her hips, and lifted her down onto the floor. Her soft laugh traveled across the deck, and every muscle in Chase's body locked up.

"What crawled up your ass, bro?" Chandler demanded.

Chase ignored him, unable to look away from the situation unfolding before him.

His oldest brother followed his gaze and chuckled. "What is little Maddie up to over there?"

"Nothing but trouble," Chase muttered.

Chandler laughed. "She's just having fun. There's nothing wrong with her dancing with some guy."

He so did not agree.

"She ain't a kid anymore," Chandler added, like Chase needed help realizing that.

Anger pricked at him. "She doesn't even know that guy."

"So?" And then he seemed to understand. "Aw, man, you've got to be shitting me."

Chase's head whipped toward his brother. Any other man would've cowered away from the dangerous look on his face, but not his brother. Nothing scared Chandler. "What?"

"Don't even try to pretend." Chandler shook his head and then laughed. "You've got it bad for Maddie."

He scowled. "You have no idea what you're talking about."

"Bullshit." Chandler propped his hip against the railing and glanced over his shoulder. "Mitch will probably beat the shit out of you."

Like I don't know that already, but thanks for pointing it out. Chase's gaze swung back to Maddie. There was still some space between her and the tool, but she was smiling at the guy—the kind of smile that was innocent and sexy as hell all at the same time, and Chase's gut clenched.

Chandler clasped his shoulder. "But I think after he knocked the crap out of you, he'd probably thank you."

Doubtful. "For what?"

His brother stared back at him like Chase was an idiot. "Maddie could end up with someone worse."

"Wow. Thanks." A wry grin tugged at his lips.

"You know what I mean. Once he gets over the idea of you and her, he'd be more than happy about it. He knows you. Trusts you."

Yeah, and that was the bitch of it. Mitch trusted Chase, so doing anything with Maddie was spitting in Mitch's face, 'cause there was no doubt in Chase's mind things would end badly. "Yeah, it's not going to happen," he said finally.

Chandler was quiet for a long moment as his gaze fixed on the swaying grape trees. "You want to tell me why?"

"Do I need to?"

There was another pause and then, "I just don't get it. Maddie has always loved you—don't give me that look.

Everyone knows it." His brother flashed a rare grin. "You two would be good together—she would be good for you."

He refused to even think about that.

"And you're good enough for her," his brother added quietly.

Chase thrust a hand through his hair. "Why are we having this conversation? Hell, if anything, her brother should be taking her little ass back to her cabin before she gets into trouble with what's-his-dick."

Chandler chuckled. "Looks like Mitch is taking his fiancée out behind the bushes."

And hell if Mitch wasn't, not that he could blame him. Chase blew out a long breath, considered heading back to the cabin . . . or sleeping in the car for the night. It was getting late and standing here, watching her—

Maddie's laughter rang out like wind chimes as she was lifted into the air, wineglass long forgotten. The guy had his arms around her waist, pulling her closer to him.

And that was it.

Chase stopped thinking. Pushing off the railing, he barely registered his brother said something taunting to his retreating back as Chase prowled across the deck and came up behind the guy, ignoring his brother's distant laughter.

For a moment, the two before Chase didn't seem to notice him, but then Maddie's glossed-over gaze drifted beyond the guy's shoulder. The tool stiffened and then turned around. One look at Chase's face struck the idiot speechless. Good.

"Maddie," Chase said, voice surprisingly calm. "It's time to go back."

She stared at him, her cheeks flushed prettily. "Why?"

His look should have said he really didn't need to explain but it was obvious she just wasn't seeing things clearly. "I seriously think it's time to call it a night."

Maddie pouted and then turned, searching for her glass. "It's still early. And I'm not ready to go back. Bobby, did you see where I put my glass? It's around here, I swear."

Her refusal must've given the little twerp courage because he planted himself in front of Maddie and Chase. "I'll make sure she gets back to her room safely tonight."

"Yeah, that's not going to happen."

Bobby-Dipshit held his ground while Maddie peered into the shadowy corners, searching for her lost glass. "She's cool, man."

"She's nothing to you." Chase brushed past the guy, leaving him standing there with his ruined plans for the evening. No way in hell if he was alive and breathing was some guy like that going to end up making Maddie a one-night stand.

Chase gently wrapped his fingers around Maddie's arm and pulled her away from where a bottle of wine was chilling in ice. "Come on, let's go back to our room."

He gave Bobby a pointed look, satisfaction settling in Chase's belly as his words sunk in and Bobby's eyebrows shot up, his hands raised in surrender as he backed away. *Yeah, game over, asshole.*

She started to protest, but then she swayed way to the left, pressing her hand to her mouth and giggling. "I may be a little tipsy. Not too much, but I think I might be well on my way."

Chase arched a brow.

Maddie giggled again as she peered up at him through thick lashes. "You look like you've sucked on something sour. What's your problem? I was just dancing and . . ."

"And what?" he growled lowly.

She scrunched her nose. "Well, I was . . . huh, I don't know."

He rolled his eyes. "Come on, let's get you to bed."

"Oh, listen to you! Ordering me to bed. For shame," she said, giggling as she wiggled free from his light grasp. "What would people think? The controversy, Chase."

"Maddie . . ."

She flounced off ahead, and he sighed, trailing after her. Surprisingly, she was heading for the stairs that led to the pathway and away from the wine, which was a good thing, he guessed.

Passing Chandler, he cut his brother a look before he could make some smartass comment. And it was on the tip of his tongue, too. One thing Chandler didn't do was relationships of any sort. His brother dated, sure, but it would be a good day in hell before the eldest brother settled down.

"Have a good night," Chandler called out, laughing.

Chase flipped him off.

She made it down one step before he swooped in, getting an arm around her narrow waist. She leaned against him, and he led her down the stairs without her falling and breaking her neck.

Getting Maddie back to the cabin was an experience in patience and reluctant amusement. Several times she broke away from him and started to roam off to God knew where. He doubted she knew. Halfway back to their cabin, she kicked off her heels. Near the cabin next to theirs, she sat down in the middle of the pathway illuminated by the pale glow of the moon.

"What are you doing?" he asked.

"Taking a break."

Shaking his head, he walked up behind her. "You haven't been walking that far."

"It seems like we've been walking forever." She tipped her back against his knees and grinned. "I'm one of those drunk girls. You know, the kind who sits down in the middle of the street? God . . . it's like I'm in college again!"

He frowned. "Did you sit in the middle of the street a lot when you were in college?"

"More times than I remember," she replied with a chuckle.

"I don't remember that."

She raised a hand and pointed at him, but her aim was wobbly, so she ended up popping herself in the face.

He winced and grabbed her small hand, steering it away from her face. "Ouch."

Maddie didn't seem to notice that she'd almost knocked out her own teeth. "*You* weren't always around, you know."

Chase fought a grin as he bent down, got his hands under her arms, and lifted her back up. "Am I going to have to carry you? If so, it would complete my badass knight-in-shining-armor act with you today."

"You are not a knight." She stumbled forward and then spun around, patting him on the chest hard enough to make him grunt. "But you kind of are. You have a good heart, Chase Gamble."

Wow. She had blown past just tipsy. "Okay. I think I might have to carry you."

She huffed. "I can walk, thank you very much. I was just tired."

"Thought you weren't tired."

"I'm not," she argued.

He stared at her.

"You're such a bore." Maddie staggered ahead and then stopped, tilting her head back on her long, graceful neck. When her hair was loose, it hung clear to her hips when she did that. "The moon is so big."

There was something big growing in his pants. And he was pretty sure that made him the worst kind of bastard. But he couldn't help it. Chase was still a man and, off-limits or not, Maddie was . . . she was just Maddie.

Looking over her shoulder, she smiled. "I'm really happy for my brother," she rambled on. "They're going to have babies, and I'll get to be an aunt. I can take them to the Smithsonian, teach them about history and . . . and stuff."

"You're going to turn those kids that don't exist yet into nerds."

She held up her finger, placing it an inch from his face, and he had an urge to lick it. "Nerds are cool. You are not."

Chase laughed as he took her hand, gently pulling her down the pathway. "What kind of stuff will you teach them?"

"Oh, you know, stuff . . . like the Civil War and how important it is to take care of our battlefields, preserve history . . . and I'll get them to volunteer."

"Will you?" They were almost to the door. Just a few more steps.

She pulled her hand free and pushed him lightly. "Yes, I will. I'm good at my job."

"I have no doubt." And he didn't. Granted, he'd never told Maddie he was proud of all she'd accomplished or how in college she'd always been on the dean's list.

Maybe he should've.

Confused by that, he followed her to the door. Once inside, she made her way to the edge of the bed and sat down heavily.

He turned on a small lamp with a fuchsia shade in the corner and then flipped the switch off on the wall. Less light was probably a good thing.

"So how are we going to do this?" She glanced at the bed and then at him. "Are we having a real sleepover?"

Chase hardened painfully at the thought of just being in bed beside her. "I'll be taking the couch."

She stared at him but said nothing. Needing to distance himself, he went over to his luggage, pulled out a pair of lightweight lounge pants and a shirt. "I'll get changed in the bathroom."

"Why?"

Was he seriously going to have to explain this to her? By her wide eyes, that would be a yes. "Get changed while I'm in there, Maddie."

Her lips thinned. "I might have drunk one . . . or four . . . too many glasses of wine, but I'm not drunk *or* stupid."

Chase was on the fence about the first. Sending her one last meaningful glance, he went into the bathroom, closed the door, and quickly changed. That was when he noticed her little bag of personal items open on the sink.

56

Toothpaste, hairbrush, a few items of makeup. Little stuff, but all hers. He reached out, running his fingers over the handle of the brush. A weird, totally inappropriate image of her stuff spread across the sink in his condo filled his head. An ache sprung in his chest, tight and familiar.

Man, he needed meds or something. It was a nice fantasy, but it was only a fantasy.

When enough time had passed, he went back into the main room. Maddie was still on the bed where he'd left her, staring at the bear rug on the floor.

He sighed. "Maddie, what are you doing?"

"That rug is really creepy, don't you think?"

Moving to the center of the room, he folded his arms over his chest. "It's not something I'd put in my place."

She winced. "I'm going to have nightmares about the thing coming alive and gnawing on my foot while I sleep. Totally ruin my pedi."

His gaze dropped to her dainty feet. He wouldn't mind gnawing on one himself. "Maddie, you should get changed for bed."

Standing up, she picked at the edge of her dress. When he'd seen her earlier, he had thought that shade of blue had been the perfect color on her.

Maddie sighed. "I sleep naked, so I didn't bring any night clothes. Didn't think it would be a problem . . ."

Oh, for fuck's sake.

Images of her glistening skin, flushed and smooth like satin, sliding under the sheets, filled his head. His body had been strung taut as a bow all night, but now his cock was throbbing. He hungered for her on a primitive, raw level. The things he'd do to her . . .

And that was why he wouldn't do anything. Not to Maddie. She was too good.

Turning away from her, he frantically searched for a resolution. "I have some shirts that will be long enough for you to wear." He started toward his luggage, the swollen member between his thighs making it hard to concentrate on anything other than what it wanted, which was to spread those pretty thighs and plunge deep inside her, over and over again. *Not gonna happen, boy, so just settle down.* He grabbed a dark shirt and turned.

Maddie stood behind him. "I'm sorry."

"Sorry for what? Getting a little tipsy?" Chase shook out the shirt. "Hold your arms up."

She obeyed, lifting them into the air. "I'm sorry about all of this." Her voice muffled as the cotton shirt got stuck for a moment over her head, and he couldn't help but grin as he tugged it down. "You must hate this," she said as her head popped through.

"Hate what?" He yanked the shirt down, and thank God, it was just as long as the dress. Sneaking his arms under the shirt, he fumbled for the zipper in the back. The sides of his arms brushed the swell of her breasts, and he stepped closer without realizing it.

"Being stuck with me," she said, tipping her head back to meet his stare.

He frowned. "I'm not stuck with you, Maddie."

She didn't say anything.

His fingers found the zipper and he pulled. The dress

eased down, pooling around her feet, and his hands . . . God damn it, his hands were on the bare skin of her back. Like he remembered, her skin was as soft as satin.

Chase needed to remove his hands pronto and step back, but she swayed forward, placing her smaller palms on his waist, her bare thighs brushing his. Then she placed her cheek against his chest and sighed.

"I've missed you," she murmured.

He felt something in his chest lurch. "Baby, how can you miss me? We see each other every day."

"I know." A tiny sigh leaked out. "But it's not the same. We're not the same. And I miss you."

God, wasn't that the truth? Ever since that night in his club, things had been different. And right now, he was frozen, caught between knowing he needed to put distance between them and wanting to hold her in his arms. And how many times had he held her like this? Not in recent years, but when she was younger, many times.

The odd, empty spot in his chest he usually ignored warmed. As a kid, he and his brothers couldn't stand to be in their cold house, surrounded by their mother's crushed dreams of marriage and their father's absence, so being around Mitch, Maddie, and their family had always eased that loneliness.

Especially Maddie. She had this way of hers, wiggling herself around his heart. Even during the times they hadn't really talked, she existed in the back of his mind like a constant ghost, haunting him.

Closing his eyes, he rested his chin atop her head. "I . . . I miss you, too."

She lifted her head and smiled sleepily, staring up at him

with so much trust in her beautiful eyes, and God, he bet she'd let him do anything to her, right here and right now. His body screamed for it, demanded it, really.

With more willpower than he knew he had, he guided her over to the heart-shaped bed, pulled back the covers, and gently sat her down. In a surprising turn of fate, she didn't argue with him but slid those curvy, sexy legs under the blanket and laid down.

"Where are you going to sleep?" she asked, lids lowering.

Chase hovered over her, drinking in the sight. He knew exactly how many freckles she had across her nose and cheeks. Twelve, to be exact. Knew that the tiny scar under her full bottom lip, a shade whiter than the rest of her skin, was from a bike accident when she was seven. Knew those lips, depending on her mood, could be so expressive.

He looked over his shoulder. The couch was long and narrow, no doubt as comfortable as sleeping on a pile of boards.

"Chase?" she whispered.

Forcing a smile, he brushed a strand of hair off her face and then, without meaning to, his hand lingered along her cheek, cupping it. She turned to the gesture and another soft sigh leaked from her parted lips. "The couch has my name on it," he said.

"There's more than enough room here." She rolled onto her side, facing him. "I don't bite."

The problem was, he kind of hoped she did. "I'm fine."

Remarkably, she was asleep before he could say anything else, which was a good thing, because if she offered the bed to him again, he wasn't sure he could refuse a second time.

Chase lowered his lips to her cheek and pressed a kiss there before backing away. Turning off the light, he went to the couch and stretched out, doing his best to get comfortable. That ache was back in his chest again, and this time, he knew it wasn't for the lack of her hugs.

It was for the lack of her in his life.

Chapter Five

With half a bottle of Tylenol trying to work its magic on the wine-induced headache, Madison winced behind her sunglasses as she shuffled alongside her mother. Touring the vineyards sounded fun, would probably have been pretty interesting, too, if she wasn't certain a psychotic drummer had taken up residency in her head.

God, she really drank a little too much last night. Dancing on a bench? Having to be escorted back to the cabin by a surprisingly rational Chase? Shamed and more than a little frustrated with herself, she kept close to her family as they piled onto the seats in the back of the bed of a cattle truck, where they'd view the vineyard up close and personal.

Bobby? Robby? Whatever his name was, he'd ended up in the other car, thank God. She couldn't even look at him without wanting to hide herself under the hay covering the bed of the truck.

Every bump went straight to Madison's temples. She gripped the seat, jaw clamped tight as the vehicle swayed along the narrow road.

Under the brim of her mother's wide straw hat, she grimaced. "You're looking a little peckish."

Before she could respond, Chad cut in with a grin. "She drank, like, twenty glasses of wine last night."

"Madison," her mother admonished, her brows slamming down.

She rolled her eyes. "I didn't drink twenty glasses."

Her father rubbed his trim beard. "How many did you drink?"

"I don't know." She glanced at a silent Chase. "Maybe four . . . ?"

Her mother gasped, but Lissa giggled as Madison's brother grinned and shook his head. "What a wino," he said.

Madison made a face and then turned. As far as the eye could see, there were grape trees and rolling hills under the bright glare of the sun and blue skies. Luckily the conversation turned from her hangover to wedding plans. Friday night, there would be a rehearsal, since the bachelor and bachelorette parties had been held the week prior. There was a busload of wedding programs that needed to be folded and, wanting to be of some use to the whole shindig, Madison offered to do it before dinner.

"Thank you!" Lissa exclaimed, obviously grateful. "You'll probably need some help. There are a lot of programs, plus the little card holders. I'm sure some of the other bridesmaids would love to help."

Being the maid of honor, she knew these were the kind of things she should be doing, and she actually wanted to. And the other girls had done so much, stepped in whenever Madison had needed their help. "It's okay. I can do it. Let them relax."

Lissa relented, but she passed a look to Mitch.

Madison loosened her grip and smoothed her hands over her denim skirt. Sitting across from her was Chase. Even though he hadn't said more than two words to her since she crawled out of bed, she could feel his eyes on her.

Last night . . . Dear God, he'd had to help her change out of her dress and she'd admitted that she slept naked. Well, she definitely added another notch to the humiliation belt. Swearing off wine forever, she stole a quick glance at him.

Their eyes locked just as the tour guide stopped by a large stone building. Everyone unloaded in a rush. Mitch and Lissa in the front, their arms snug around each other's waists. Her parents were just as cuddly. Like Chase had said earlier, they were treating the trip like a honeymoon. They hadn't had a real one after they married, so Madison was glad to see them having so much romance and fun.

"Here," said a deep voice.

Madison looked up, surprised to find Chase beside her, holding a bottle of water. She took it, offering a tentative smile. "Thank you."

He shrugged. "I've seen many hangovers worse than what you have, but the water should help."

Chase would know, she thought, unscrewing the lid and taking a drink. Besides running three clubs where liquor poured from the ceilings, he'd been quite the partier in college, and then there had been his mother . . . Chase and his brothers had probably learned how to treat a hangover at an early age. She always found it strange that Chase had gone into the nightclub business, but he was clearly determined to be "like father, like son," she supposed. His dad had owned dozens of bars and nightclubs. It seemed only natural that one of the brothers would've followed suit.

But Chase . . . He wasn't like his father, not really. He wasn't as cold as the elder Gamble or as selfish. A fine shudder rolled through Madison as she recalled the few times she'd been in the Gamble house. Once when she was just a kid and then when she'd been seventeen. Both times, the house had been sterile and frigid. His mother had been a lifeless shell, living from one wine bottle and prescription pill to the next. The woman had loved the boys' father to the point of death and their father . . . he hadn't seemed to care.

Discreetly peeking at Chase from behind her sunglasses, she noticed again how out of the three brothers, Chase was the one who resembled his father, but even with the clubs, the girls, and the success, he was the least like him.

He just couldn't seem to stop acting like he was.

When he glanced at her, she looked straight ahead. Why was she even thinking about this stuff? It didn't matter, and if she didn't start paying attention, she'd tumble right down the narrow steps the guide was leading them down into the wine cellar where thousands of bottles were racked and stocked from the floor to the ceiling.

Something was different about Chase today as he joked with his brothers and Mitch. Like a tension in his shoulders that hadn't been there yesterday morning had set in. She hoped it wasn't from sleeping on that terrible couch.

The air was several degrees cooler in the wine cellar, and she rubbed her arms, chasing the chill away. Since wine storage wasn't of much interest to her, she roamed off, following the maze of bottles.

Good Lord, if she were claustrophobic, being down here would be a problem with how tight and narrow and tall the racks were.

Her flip-flops smacked on the cement floor as she tried to read the names on the bottles. Most of them were unpronounceable to her and honestly, she'd go to the grave before she had another sip of that stuff.

The voices of the group faded off as her fingers trailed along the chilled bottles. She wasn't a big drinker, obviously. Last night had been out of the norm.

Stopping at the edge of the rack, she glanced over her shoulder, suddenly realizing she couldn't hear anyone anymore. Frowning, she backtracked to where she thought she'd left them, but no one was there.

"Crap," she muttered, hurrying down an aisle.

This wasn't happening. They did not leave her. Tightening her grip on the water bottle, she barreled around the corner, smacked right off a hard chest, and almost landed on her ass.

Chase snatched her arm before she ended up on her rear. "Whoa. You okay?"

Blinking, she nodded. "I didn't know you were there." She took a step back, ignoring the sudden increase in her heart rate. Her reaction was ridiculous. "Why are you here?"

He cocked his head to the side. "The group is moving on to lunch."

"Oh?" Since she wasn't bouncing around in that horrible truck, her stomach perked up happily.

A half grin appeared. "It's a picnic, I hear, out in the actual vineyards."

That sounded incredibly tasty and romantic. "Well, we better hurry, then."

Stepping aside, Chase let her walk by. He followed behind her silently, and she wished he'd say something. Anything. But then again, she had no idea what to say, either. The awkwardness that had developed between them sucked. Proof positive why friends of any sort should never cross that invisible line . . . At least not unless they planned on crossing all the way.

When they reached the entrance, Chase swore under his breath. "Where in the hell is everyone?"

A horrible sensation snaked its way through the pit of her stomach as she glanced up and down the empty aisles. There was no sound other than Chase's soft breath and her pounding heart.

"They didn't . . . ?" She trailed off, unable to accept what was happening.

"No." He edged around her and pounded up the steps. Another loud curse and banging caused her to wince.

Madison found him at the top of the stairs, his hands on his hips. "Please don't say what I think you're going to say."

"We're locked in." Disbelief colored Chase's tone.

"You have got to be kidding." She squeezed past him and tried the door, jiggling the handle. Nothing. She wanted to smack her head off the door but figured since her headache had finally eased, that was not a good idea. "They left us."

Chase leaned against the cool cement blocks, closing his eyes. "They have to realize we're missing. They'll come back. Soon. It won't be that long."

Boy, she hoped so. She was already colder than a witch's

tit, but as five minutes passed and then ten, it wasn't looking like a rescue was going to happen anytime soon.

Madison dropped down on the step, chasing away the goose bumps on her bare legs with her hands. "You know, I'm kind of offended that no one has even realized we're not with them."

He chuckled and settled onto the step above her, leaning forward and crossing his hands on his bent knees. His face was nearly eye-level with hers, so now she didn't have to tilt her head to talk to him. "Yeah, it does wonders for your self-esteem, doesn't it?"

"I bet they're enjoying their lunch, too. Eating finger sandwiches, drinking club soda, and thinking, 'Hmm, the group seems different, but oh, never mind, we have pickled eggs!'"

Chase's deep, husky laugh warmed her belly. "This reminds me of something."

At first, she didn't know where he was going with that statement as she pulled the sunglasses off her head and placed them next to her water on the top ledge. And then it hit her.

Oh, for the love of all things holy in this world.

"You were seven," he said, humor lacing his voice.

She lowered her head in shame. Chase had this wonderfully selective memory when it came to remembering the most humiliating moments in her life.

"And Mitch and I were going to the park to play a game of basketball and you wanted to go, but Mitch wouldn't let you." Another chuckle filled the pause. "So, you decided to retaliate."

"Can we talk about something else?"

He ignored her. "By stuffing yourself in a chest in the tree house—what the hell did you hope to gain by that?"

Her cheeks burned. "I was hoping that you guys would come back and miss me, and then you'd feel bad for not letting me play with you. Yeah, I know, not the smartest plan, but I was a kid."

Chase shook his head and a lock of dark hair fell forward over his forehead. "You could've killed yourself."

"Well, I didn't."

"Except we thought you went to the neighbors' house," he added, frowning now. "Man, you had to be in that chest for hours."

She had. Luckily it had a huge rusted-out hole in the side, but something had gone wrong when she had closed the trunk. It had locked on her. Even with her scrawny arms, she couldn't reach the latch from the inside. So she had stayed in that damn chest, helpless as night fell and she felt like spiders were crawling over her. She remembered crying for what felt like days and then finally falling asleep, positive she was going to die alone.

"When your dad realized you weren't at the neighbors' and no one had seen you since we'd left for the park, I thought he was going to lock us in one of his bomb shelters."

Imagining how angry her father must've been, she laughed. Half the reason why she'd been able to tail them so much as a kid was the fact her parents had put the fear of God in Mitch and the Gamble brothers. If Madison wanted to play with them, she got to play and set the rules.

Too bad it didn't work that way now.

"You found me," she said, closing her eyes.

"I did."

"How?" she asked. It was the one thing she'd never figured out.

Chase was quiet for so long, she thought he might not remember. "We searched everywhere—my brothers and your family. They'd been in the tree house, but I don't know why I checked it again. I saw that damn chest we used to sit on and looked in that hole. I saw your red jumper and about had a heart attack. I called your name and you didn't answer." A heartbeat passed. "I thought you were dead in there. I had to use that busted old hammer to pry the lock open." He took a deep breath. "You scared the hell out of me."

She bit her lip as she remembered him picking her up and carrying her back to the house. "Sorry. I didn't mean to scare you guys."

"I know. You were just a kid."

There was a pause and then she said, "Sorry about last night."

He shrugged it off.

"No. Really. I was pretty blitzed, and I vaguely remember hitting myself in the face."

The skin at the corners of his eyes crinkled as he chuckled. "You did do that."

"So embarrassing," she muttered. "Anyway, I'm sorry you had to deal with that."

"Don't be. It was fun."

"Fun?"

He nodded. "You were pretty keen on the moon and

70

teaching Mitch and Lissa's kids about volunteering and *stuff*—lots of *stuff*."

Madison grinned.

There was a drawn-in breath and then, "So, you sleep naked?"

Aw, man . . .

"All the time?" Curiosity marked his tone.

She sighed. "All the time."

"Nice."

Peeking over her shoulder at him, she raised her brows. He winked. And then he said nothing else. In the silence that followed, she searched for something to say. "How're the clubs going?"

"Good." He folded muscular arms over his chest. "I'm thinking about opening a fourth in Virginia."

"Really? Wow. That's a lot to handle."

"I don't know. Nothing is in stone yet, but it's looking good. There's Father's clubs, but they seem to be doing well under their own ownership. Never thought to step in and buy them out from the management he had in place. I rather prefer having my own. It means more that way, like it wasn't handed to me . . ." His gaze dropped to where she was rubbing her calves, and she stopped, flushing.

Chase cleared his throat. "Mitch was telling me that you petitioned for more funding for the volunteer department and succeeded."

At the beginning of the year, like every place in the world, the Smithsonian was facing budget cuts, and volunteer services was one of the first departments to take a hit. It had taken months to petition, blood and quite a bit of frustrated tears, to finally be awarded a grant that allowed them to continue operating.

Madison nodded.

His eyes warmed with pride, and she felt all kinds of warm and fuzzy from seeing that. "That's really good."

Never comfortable with compliments, she flushed and looked away. "It took a lot of work, but I enjoyed it."

"It's good . . . seeing you doing something you enjoy."

Her chin jerked toward him as she tried to decipher why he had said that, but then realized he probably meant it exactly how it sounded. "Same for you."

Chase nodded and then took a deep breath. Madison steeled herself. She knew that sound, knew he was going to say something she probably wouldn't like.

"About what happened . . . yesterday afternoon . . . ?" A muscle pulsed in his jaw. "I shouldn't have left like that."

Surprised, she stared for several moments and then found her voice. "No, you shouldn't have."

He took that in stride. "It did happen, and I shouldn't have told you it didn't."

She wondered if there was an apocalypse going on outside. Comets falling from the sky. Poles shifting. Icebergs melting. Her parents would be thrilled.

The tips of his cheeks flushed. "And I'm sorry. I shouldn't have—"

"Don't," she said, on her feet before she realized it. In the cramped space, there was very little room between them, and her anger was like a third person crowding them in. "Don't tell me you shouldn't have done it."

His eyes went wide and then narrowed. "Maddie—"

"And stop calling me that." Her hands balled into fists. "I think you've made it perfectly clear how unattractive you find me."

"Whoa. Wait." He threw up his hands. "This has nothing to do with that."

She huffed. "Yeah, because when you're attracted to someone, you actually enjoy kissing them and afterward, you don't act like you kissed Adolf Hitler."

His lips twitched as if he were trying not to smile, and he stood, too. "For one thing, that's not how I acted. And secondly, I don't want to hear 'kissing' and 'Hitler' in the same sentence ever again, because now I'm picturing you with that little Hitler mustache."

"Shut up."

"And that's not hot—not hot at all."

His tone was light, playful even, but now her face was burning, and there was no escaping him. "Whatever."

Anger darkened the hue of his eyes, turning them cobalt blue, and the mischievous glimmer was gone. "Talking about this—trying to be a decent guy about the situation— was obviously a mistake."

"Just like kissing me was yesterday, right?"

"Obviously," he shot back.

Madison flinched, and for a second, she thought she saw regret flicker in his eyes, but then he looked away. Everything came to a head in an instant. Years of confusion and regret mixed together to form a nasty ball of emotion. She tipped her chin up. "Tell me, do you call your other girlfriends after you make out with them and apologize for your drunken behavior?"

The muscle in his jaw popped out.

Undaunted, she took a step forward, getting right in his face. "I bet you don't. They probably get phone calls that don't include an apology and flowers instead of being left behind like discarded trash."

Anger flared in his eyes. "You're not discarded trash."

"Yeah, I guess I'm just not good enough, then. But hey, be happy, because soon we'll have our own rooms and won't have to keep *apologizing* to each other." She turned away and walked down the steps to find a damn chest to hide in, because tears were burning her eyes and she knew how jealous she sounded.

She was making a fool out of herself. Again.

Madison made it down one step before Chase's hand caught her arm and whipped her back around. He glowered at her. "You don't have a freaking clue, do you?"

She tried to pull her arm free, but he held on. "A clue about what?"

"It has nothing to do with you being good enough or me being attracted to you. Not at all."

"I'm not sure who you're trying to convince, bud. I think your track record with me speaks for itself."

One second she was in the middle of the step and the next her back was against the wall and Chase's body was flush to hers, meeting in all the right places.

"Tell me," he said, voice low and thick. "Does it seem like I'm not attracted to you?"

Oh, oh yeah, he was *definitely* attracted to her. The breath went out of her lungs and her mouth felt dry. Every inch of his body pressed against hers, and she could feel his erection, long and thick against her belly. Electricity hummed over her entire body.

"I'm . . . I'm starting to get the picture," she said. "It's a pretty big picture."

Any other day, Chase might have laughed, but not now. He was furious and there was more, but she wasn't afraid. Fear and Chase's name were two things that would never go together.

She tried to swallow, to take a breath, but her eyes met his, and there was nothing but aching intensity in his gaze. And she was drawn in, swept away.

Maybe she really didn't have a freaking clue.

Chase's warm hand slid up her bare arm, to the edge of the tiny strap on her tank top. A wave of small bumps followed his touch, and when his fingers edged under that fragile slip of material, her legs would've cut out from under her if he hadn't been pressed so tightly against her body.

He dipped his head, placing his mouth to the space below her ear. He nipped her there, just a tiny bite that sent a wave of heat through her veins. And then his lips moved lower, leaving a hot trail behind. "You drive me insane, absolutely freaking insane. Do you know that? I bet you do."

Hushing the voice in the back of her head that screamed and ranted a thousand warnings, she gripped his shoulders as her head fell back against the wall, giving him all the access he wanted.

And he did want.

Those firm lips of his traveled back up her throat to pause above her own. Her chest rose sharply, and his other hand fell to her hip, fingers digging into the denim as he held her in place.

Their eyes locked.

"We shouldn't be doing this," he growled, and then he kissed her deeply, stealing her breath as he pulled back, nipping at her lower lip. "Not because I find you unattractive." His pelvis thrust against hers as if to drive his point home. "And not because I don't think you're good enough. You're too good, Maddie, too damn good, and that's the problem."

Madison didn't know what he meant by that, and she couldn't breathe as his thick thigh pushed her legs apart and she gasped as the rough material met her bare, sensitive skin. Finding out why they weren't supposed to be doing exactly what they were doing took second seat to the ache in her core and the wild rush of feelings she'd harbored for this man for years.

"God," Chase groaned as his hips pressed forward. "We're really going to have to do something about the not-wearing-panties thing, Maddie. Seriously."

She closed her eyes and arched her back as her hips swiveled, the friction from his thigh and her own eagerness igniting a fire deep inside her. When she spoke, her voice was breathy and unrecognizable. "Do what?"

Both of his hands grasped her hips as he lifted her onto his thigh more fully, and she could feel him burning through the thin cotton of her shirt.

"This is crazy," he said, which wasn't much of an answer. Not that she cared.

His eyes were on fire as he pulled her up against him and

kissed her so deeply she felt like he was devouring the very taste of her.

She looped her arms around his neck, her fingers digging into the soft hair at the nape of his neck. Her body moved against his, and all she could hope for, all she wanted, was for him to not stop. To never stop.

For him to prove what his body was saying meant more than his words.

Discarded trash? Those words rang in his ears like a drum. His father had left his mom behind like that—something to rot away in their million-dollar home, surrounded by jewels, furs, pool boys, and everything the woman could want except the one thing she needed—her husband's love and fidelity. Maddie would never, could never be discarded trash.

Chase sucked in a ragged breath a second before she fastened his mouth to hers. This was insane, but his control had snapped somewhere between her accusing him of not being attracted to her and her fiery show of temper.

He couldn't stop now, knew that he didn't want to, not when she was so warm and eager against him. His sex surged even harder as her hips rocked and she made those breathy sounds against his lips.

His hand trailed to her breast, felt the pebbling of her nipple, and all gentlemanly whims went right out the damn cellar along with his common sense.

Chase could feel her body tremble as he kissed her. Even though he was hard as granite in his jeans, he struggled to stop this catastrophe from happening. Because in the end, could he really have her? She was so far above him, and she didn't even see it.

But it was like he didn't have control of his hands. His finger nudged under the straps of her tank top, lowering them down her arms, baring the soft swells to the cold air and his hungry gaze.

"God, you're beautiful." He cupped her breast, losing a little more of himself in her softness as his thumb brushed over the hardened peak. "So perfect . . ."

Her breathy moan of denial shattered him as his hand traveling farther south, beyond the flare of her hip.

Then her back arched, the skirt sliding farther up her thighs. "Please, Chase, please."

How was he supposed to deny her? How could he ever?

His head dipped to one rosy tip, his tongue flicked out, and he drew her into his mouth. Her skin was too tempting to resist. The taste of her . . . blew his mind.

Chase's hand teased under her skirt, along the curve of her taut ass, to the moist, slick petals of her sex. He drew his finger along her core, and she felt like satin. He was in awe, enthralled and captured by her. Honestly nothing new, but . . .

Christ, she was soft and yielding in his arms, and so very damn perfect.

And he wanted her, all of her—

Footsteps on the other side of the door knocked him out of this fantasy like being blasted with a nuclear weapon.

Jerking back, he caught Maddie before she tumbled down the stairs. She stared up at him, the look on her face so shell-shocked and demanding that he wanted to bar the damn door shut and do this, keep doing this.

In a miraculous feat, he readjusted her clothing seconds before the door swung open. Spinning on the step, he used his body to block hers, giving her time to regain her composure.

The tour guide stood there, holding a key. Behind him, Chandler arched a knowing brow. Great.

"Ah," Chandler said, "there you are. I'm guessing the little shadow behind you is Madison? We've been looking everywhere for you two."

"Well, we've been *here* the whole time. *Locked in.*" He said it with emphasis and glanced over his shoulder, finding a wide-eyed and flushed face staring back. Steeling himself, he faced his brother's mocking stare. "Took long enough."

Chandler snickered. "For some reason, I have the exact opposite impression."

Chase ignored his brother's snide comment. He was more concerned with how in the hell he was going to keep his hands off Maddie now.

Chapter Six

What the hell just happened? Madison was lost. One moment they were arguing and the next, they were kissing and doing way, way more than that. Really hot stuff that had strung her tight as a bow, so close to shattering, and then . . .

Then Chase's brother showed up. *Awkward* wasn't even the word for that.

She was still in a daze when they were ushered to the hillside where the picnic had been set up. Chase had returned to stoic silence while his older brother had a smirk affixed to his handsome face the entire way back, and Madison . . . She honestly didn't know what to do.

She felt like a bipolar zombie—a horny bipolar zombie.

Her mom rushed up and squeezed the daylights out of her the moment she was spotted. Madison almost took a hat to the eye. "We were so worried, honey! I thought you fell off the truck or something!"

Squeezing her mom back, she reassured her. "I'm fine. Just got locked in the wine cellar."

"Oh, that's terrible!"

Her father frowned. "Actually, in the event of nuclear fallout, the wine cellar may be the best place."

"Da-ad." Madison groaned.

Mitch grinned from his seat next to Lissa. "At least you had Chase to keep you company. Couldn't have been that bad and hey, you didn't kill each other."

Madison stiffened.

Strolling past her, Chandler glanced over his shoulder and winked before adding, "Which makes one wonder what they *did* do to each other."

Tugging down her hair to hide her flaming cheeks, she shrugged and settled on a blanket, busying herself with what was left of the food. Right now, surrounded by family and friends, she couldn't even begin to analyze what had happened, but she couldn't stop herself from checking out how Chase was hanging in there.

He was over with his brothers, his long legs stretched out in front of him, smiling now like he hadn't a freaking care in the world.

Okay. So this could be good. At least he wasn't brooding and coming up with an apology. Her heart flip-flopped. If he wasn't coming up with an apology, what did that mean? That he didn't regret what happened? That maybe there could be some sort of future? That maybe she was jumping way ahead of herself? But it was hard not to when she'd loved him for so long.

God, she sounded like a thirteen-year-old. "FML," she muttered.

"What, honey?" her mom questioned.

"Nothing—nothing at all."

After the picnic, the rest of the tour set into motion. Thankfully, she wasn't left behind again . . . *Or maybe not thankfully*, she thought as she glanced over at Chase for the hundredth time.

When everyone departed from the truck and headed back to their cabins to rest up before the formal dinner that evening, Madison headed toward the main lodge to knock out the wedding programs. Hopefully the mindless task would get her brain back on track. And it was probably a good idea she wasn't going back to the cabin. Being alone with Chase again so soon would likely end in disaster. She already had a mad case of nerves, having no idea how he was going to act or how she should behave. Would they argue? Would they act like nothing happened? Or would they pick up where they left off?

Door number three, please.

Before Madison made it to the steps leading to the sprawling porch, her mother wrapped an arm around her waist. "Honey, are you feeling okay?"

As frazzled as she was, the truth was bursting to come out. Well, at least a half truth. They were far enough away from the rest of the group for some privacy, but she kept her voice low. "I really don't know, Mom."

Her mom took off her hat and smoothed her hands over the wispy dark hairs sticking out haphazardly. "Is it the wedding? Work?"

"No." Madison laughed. "I'm happy for Mitch and Lissa. It's not that at all. And work is perfect."

"Then what is it?" She clasped Madison's hand. "You haven't been yourself since you arrived."

She wanted so badly to confide in someone, but what could she tell her mother? She'd die before she admitted what had happened in the wine cellar.

"It's really nothing." She smiled and then her stomach dropped as she caught a glimpse of Chase stretching. In the afternoon sun, he looked amazing. His shirt rode up, revealing the dip and roll of his abs. She had to tear her greedy gaze away.

Her mom may say and think some crazy stuff at times, but man was she observant. "Yes, I see."

"You see what?" Madison frowned.

Her mom chuckled softly. "Chase—it's always Chase."

As offensive as the statement was, there wasn't anything Madison could say. Too nervous—too anxious—about what had happened, what might happen between them, she kept her lips glued shut.

"You two have played cat and mouse for far too long," her mother said softly.

More like they played cat and cat. Madison shook her head in denial.

"Honey, I know your heart has always belonged to that Gamble boy, from the moment you started seeing him as something other than Mitch's friend—which I think was when you turned ten." Mrs. Daniels glanced over to where he stood with the guys. She tilted her head to the side. "But he's always seen his father in himself. Poor boy has no idea that he's nothing like that jackass."

"Mom!"

"What?" She laughed. "That man was a horrible father and worse husband. What that boy needs—what every Gamble boy needs—is a good woman to show him he's worth loving."

Madison opened her mouth to change the subject, but

something else entirely came out. "He'll never see himself as anything different, and he'll never see me as anything other than Mitch's sister."

"No, my dear, he already sees you as something other than Mitch's sister. He just doesn't realize it yet."

Her mother's words lingered long after Madison settled into the small room in the back of the main lodge, seated on the floor, legs tucked under her. Two heavy boxes sat in front of her. One full of programs and another stocked with little cards and holders.

Maybe she should've asked for help . . . She was going to be here all night.

Glancing at the deer head mounted on the wall, she shuddered. Sighing, she reached for the programs and began tri-folding them.

He just doesn't realize it yet.

Could that seriously be the only thing holding him back after all these years? He wanted her, cared for her, but hadn't come to accept it all yet? There was no way she believed that. And she also didn't think it was his father's influence. Either you wanted someone or you didn't. In her mind, there was no in between.

She'd considered calling Bridget, but her friend would just rant and rave over how idiotic Madison was being, which she probably deserved. Doing the non-platonic thing with Chase was stupid. But damn it, she had no willpower when it came to him.

There was a neat stack of ten folded programs by the time someone knocked on the closed door. A second later, it swung open, and Chase stood in the doorway. "Hey."

Shocked to find the object of her angst standing in front of her, all she could do was stare and remember how freaking wonderful he'd felt pressed against her. "Hey?"

Running a hand through his dark hair, he squinted. "Your mother thought you could use some help."

Damn that meddlesome woman.

Taking a deep breath, she plotted about a thousand ways to stitch her mom's mouth shut. "It's okay. I got this. I'm sure there are other things you'd rather be doing."

He raised one brow suggestively and she blushed. And now she was thinking there were things she'd rather be doing, too. Damn him.

He motioned at the full boxes. "From up here, it looks like you need help."

She shrugged as she folded a program, ducking her head and letting her hair shift forward and cover her flaming red face.

Inching into the room, he nudged the door shut. "At the rate you're going, you'll be here until the wedding."

"Hardy-har-har." She watched him sit down on the other side of the boxes. "Chase, I appreciate this . . . but you don't have to."

He shrugged and grabbed a program. A frown creased his forehead. "What the hell?" Turning over the stark white paper with crimson lettering, he shook his head. "This layout makes no sense."

Laughing softly, she set hers aside and leaned forward. "See these faint dots?" When he nodded, she sat back and picked up her own. "You have to fold them at the dots, going in a different way, like a pamphlet. See?"

It took Chase a couple of tries before he got the edges to line up perfectly. As she watched his nimble fingers slide along the crease of the second program, her cheeks heated.

He looked up, fingers pausing. "So now that I'm here, you're just going to sit there and . . . stare at me?"

Madison blinked and snatched another program. "I'm not staring at you."

"Sure." He drew the word out.

"Certain you don't have something better to do?" Dividing the programs into halves, she again wanted to strangle her mom.

"Better than annoying you? There's no such thing."

Madison tried to ignore the teasing tone to his words, but it was hard. A small grin broke free and after a couple of moments, they fell into an easy, companionable silence as they worked on the programs.

The quiet was broken by Chase's low chuckle, drawing her attention. "What?" she asked, wondering what she had done now.

"It's just strange seeing you do this. Crafts aren't your thing."

Relaxing, she steadied the growing pile between them. "You never struck me as a craft guy, either."

He laughed again. "I have no idea what I'm doing."

"You're making sure that Mitch and Lissa's wedding goes off without any problems."

"And helping you."

Madison smiled at that. "And helping me. By the way, I'm really grateful you are helping, because this would've taken me forever." Pausing, she placed another on the stack and reached for one more. "But I'm sorry my mom conned you into doing this."

Chase's fingers stilled over the program, and his gaze met hers. It was crazy. Dressed down in worn blue jeans and a black shirt, he was the most beautiful man she'd ever seen. And the moment was sort of perfect.

Even with the deer head staring over his shoulder like a total creeper.

His gaze moved to the program in his hands. "Your mom did mention you were doing this now."

His sentence seemed loaded, like she was missing the punch line or something. Tilting her head to the side, she waited. "Okay?"

"But she didn't ask me." The tips of his cheekbones flushed. "I figured you could use the help."

Her mouth opened but nothing came out. Sure, he was just helping her fold programs out of the goodness of his heart, so it wasn't a ringing declaration of love, but still . . .

Chase cleared his throat. "And with all this wine laying around, someone needs to keep an eye on you."

Madison laughed. "I'm not a wino."

"You were last night."

"Was not!"

He arched a brow. "You were dancing on a bench with some tool."

Shaking her head, she smiled. "His name is Bobby."

"I think his name is Rob."

"Oh." She bit down on her lip. "Same difference."

He leaned forward, tapping her knee with his knuckles. "And you sat down in the middle of the pathway."

She remembered. "I was tired."

"And you started talking about how big the moon was." He sat back, grinning. And suddenly . . . God, suddenly it was five years ago and everything . . . everything was normal between them.

Her chest ached, but in a good way.

"It was like you'd never seen the moon before. Surprised you still don't think it's a ball of cheese in the sky."

She threw her folded program at him. "I'm not five, Chase!"

He picked up the paper. "But you were that tipsy."

Giggling at his comment, she grabbed the box of programs and realized it was empty. Scooting over, she reached into the other one and pulled out a dozen place-card holders. Disappointment swelled when she realized they'd be done within an hour.

Madison also remembered what she'd said to him last night as he held her so tenderly in his arms, which was proof that she hadn't been that drunk.

She had admitted that she missed him—missed this. Just being together, teasing each other or sitting in comfortable silence. Back in the day, they could go for hours like this. It was why for the longest time, she believed they were meant to be together.

Seemed silly now and maybe even a little sad, but she didn't want this moment to end. Most importantly, she didn't want to miss him anymore.

* * *

Chase watched her stick the little cards into the holders, wondering what had caused the glimpse of sadness that had flashed across her face. The smile was back now, and she was telling him about the project she was delving into at work. He lo—liked her like this best.

He could easily see her with someone, just sitting around, shooting the shit, and still being incredibly sexy. Maddie had this ease about her, a natural charm that drew people in. Some guy was going to be a lucky son of a bitch one day.

The cold slice of air that came out of nowhere and shot down his neck was hard to ignore.

Pushing those thoughts away, he told her about the couple his manager had caught last weekend in the storage room. "Stefan got an eyeful when he went back to get fresh towels."

Madison tipped her head back and laughed. "And this was at Komodo? Don't they have to go through the employee lounge for that? How did they get back there?"

"One of the waitresses left the door unlocked." He grinned as her laugh bubbled up again. "Stefan said they had their iPhones out and were filming the whole thing."

"Wow." She snickered. "Amazing multitasking skills."

"Jealous?"

Her eyes rolled. "Yeah, there's nothing more romantic than getting it on while someone is shoving a phone camera in your face."

An image of Maddie under him, naked and writhing, getting it on with a camera, and then without the camera, flashed in his head.

Yeah, not romantic, but sexy as hell. It suddenly felt stifling in the small room, and he tugged at his shirt collar.

Maddie's brows furrowed. "What are you thinking about?"

"You don't even want to know."

A sweet, hot flush swept over her cheeks, and she quickly returned her attention to sticking the cards in the holders. It didn't seem possible, but the swelling between his legs was increasing. Jesus. H. Christ.

Chase stretched out his legs. Didn't help. "So . . ."

She peeked up. "So what?"

"So when are we going to be doing this for *your* wedding?"

For a long moment, long enough to realize what a crap hole he'd just stepped into, she said nothing as she stared at him. Chase started to laugh it off, but then she spoke.

"I don't know if I'll get married."

A real fucked-up part of him shouted with glee and that was wrong, because she wasn't his, she would never be, and he wanted her happy. And Maddie could never be happy alone forever.

"You'll get married, Maddie."

Flecks of green churned in her eyes. "Don't patronize me, Chase."

Leaning back, he held up his hands. "I'm not patronizing you. I'm just being realistic."

She whipped a holder out of the box and slammed the card into the poor thing. "Can you read the future? No. I didn't think so."

"I don't know why you're getting so bent out of shape." He reached over and swiped the card holder out of her hand before she bent it. "There's just no way that some guy is not going to fall head over heels in love with you. You'll have a big wedding like this, a great honeymoon, and have two kids . . ."

Damn, those words felt like nails coming back up his throat. And hell, they seemed to piss her off more.

Rising to her knees, she grabbed the stack of programs and placed them in their box. "I'll get married when you get married."

Chase let out a startled laugh. "Bullshit."

She shot him a glare as she started putting the card holders into the box. "What? You're above love and marriage?"

"I'm just not that stupid."

Her indignant huff was a clear warning. "That's right. Just sticking your dick wherever you want is good enough for you?"

Worked for his father . . . Well, not really. He watched her for a few seconds, then grabbed the box and pulled it away.

On her knees, she stopped with two card holders in her little fists. Déjà vu swept over him. Except Maddie had been six, and instead of those silver stands, she'd held two massacred Barbies that he and Mitch had cut the heads off of.

Chase laughed.

Her eyes flared green. "What's so funny?"

"Nothing," he said, sobering quickly.

Maddie's eyes narrowed. "Give me back the box."

"No."

"Give me back the box, or I will throw these in your face."

He doubted she'd do that. Well, he hoped. "What's your deal? I don't see why you're getting so worked up over my saying some guy will fall in love with you."

"Do you think it has anything to do with the fact that a couple of hours ago, I was half naked in your arms and we were seconds away from going at it against a wall?" Suddenly, her eyes popped wide and cheeks flushed. "Forget it—forget I even brought it up."

Something in his chest swelled, because even with his thick skull, he got why she was angry, but then the feeling deflated, because it didn't matter. "Aw, hell, Maddie . . ."

"I said forget it." She stood and relatively gently placed the last of the card holders in the box. "Thanks for your help."

"Damn it." He placed the box aside and shot to his feet, catching her before she made it to the door. Her eyes dropped to his hand and then flicked back to his face. "What happened between us—"

"Obviously meant nothing," she cut in. "You were just looking for a place to stick—"

"Don't ever say that," he growled, now pissed off just as much as she was. "You're not someone I'd be looking to do that with. Got that?"

Maddie blinked once and then twice. Wrenching her arm free, she swallowed. "Yeah, I think I got that."

Before he could say another word, she stormed out of the room, slamming the door in his face. Minutes went by as he stared at the space where she'd stood. When it finally sunk in why she was pissed with that last line, how she'd probably perceived what he'd said, Chase cursed again.

Thrusting a hand through his hair, he looked down at the neatly folded wedding programs and then to the door. It was better if she believed he didn't want her. Maybe even better if she believed he did but just for sex, because if he were with her, he'd break her heart.

Chapter Seven

Madison was full of restless energy when she returned to the cabin, relieved to find Chase hadn't somehow beaten her back. There were still two hours left before dinner, and she needed time to work off the anger and pent-up frustration.

Things had been going great between them, and then he had to bring up getting married, going as far as to say that she would end up with another man. Didn't he see how cruel that was after what they'd almost done? After what she'd wanted from him for years?

Eyeing the running shoes in her suitcase, she disregarded them for the massive bathtub. She needed chocolate, too, but she'd have to wait for later for that comfort. Stripping off her clothes, she stormed into the bathroom, resisting the urge to slam the door. What was the point when the only things that would hear her were the damn woodchucks outside?

And why was she so ticked off? Nothing had changed between them. Sure, they had shared two moments of pure insanity, but things were the way they'd always been. Chase just didn't want her—not badly enough and not enough to get over whatever reasons he had for not being with her.

Part of her knew it had something to do with his parents' relationship and not really her at all. All the Gamble boys seemed a little damaged. Chad was too carefree, not taking a damn thing in life seriously. Chandler only did one-night stands, and Chase . . . Chase was the playboy. He liked relationships, but he just never allowed them to last beyond his self-imposed three-month marker. Short and sweet, he liked to joke.

Groaning, she ducked her head under the frothy bubbles overflowing the tub and stayed there until her lungs burned. Bubbles lapped at the edge of the garden tub as she resurfaced, pushing long strands of hair out of her face.

"Maddie, are you in there?" Chase's deep voice boomed through the closed bathroom door.

Her eyes widened as her gaze darted around the bathroom. Had she locked the door? And why in the hell did she leave the towel all the way over there, folded neatly on the shelf above the toilet? She gripped the edge of the tub, wondering if she should pretend to be asleep.

Like that was a stellar plan.

And like all stellar plans, it backfired in her face.

The bathroom door swung open, and Chase's broad shoulders filled the gap. Her mother would've called those shoulders door busters and damn if she wasn't right.

Madison squeaked and frantically started moving the bubbles up over her chest. Seconds later she realized how stupid that was, considering he'd seen her goodies only a few hours ago, but hell, she wasn't holding peep shows.

"Why did you bust in here?" she demanded, striving to

sound calm and unaffected by the fact he was near and she was naked.

Chase folded his arms. "I called for you, but you didn't answer."

"So the next logical step was to bust into the bathroom?"

He shrugged. "I was worried you were hurt."

"In the bathroom?"

"With you, anything is possible." He stared at her, not even attempting to look anywhere else like most guys would. But Chase wasn't most guys. He was a walking contradiction.

Her gaze narrowed. "Gee. Thanks."

Chase said nothing as he stalked into the bathroom and leaned against the his-and-hers sinks.

Madison's heart rate skyrocketed into uncharted territories. "Um, can I help you with something?"

His lashes lowered, and she knew where his gaze went—to the rapidly thinning bubbles—and heat zinged through her veins. "I'm not sure," he said finally. Then his eyes settled back on her face. "We need to talk."

"Right at this very moment?"

"What's wrong with right now?"

Was he daft? "I'm in the bathtub, Chase, in case you haven't noticed."

"Oh, I've noticed." His voice dropped low, husky, and sexy as hell.

And her body went right into take-me-now land. God, there needed to be an anti-sex pill or something for when she was around him. She eyed the towel across the room and sighed. "Can it wait until I'm done?" They had a few hours left before dinner, so time wasn't an issue. Being in the bathtub was, however.

"I've seen you naked before, Maddie."

Her mouth dropped open. "You have not seen me completely naked, thank you very much."

His eyes glittered. "Actually, once before I have, when you were, like, five. You ran through the house buck-ass naked when you had chicken pox."

"Oh, dear God, why do you remember these things?" She was going to drown herself, right here in the tub.

A half smile appeared. "It was kind of traumatizing."

"Yeah, well, *this* is traumatizing, so we're even." Since it appeared he wasn't leaving, she scooped more bubbles over her breasts. "Okay. What do we need to talk about?"

"You. Me. What's been going on between us." He said it so matter-of-factly she thought she'd misheard him at first.

But she hadn't.

She sunk her hands under the water as she stared at him. He seemed transfixed by where her hands had gone. "There's something going on between us?"

Chase's expression was unreadable as he nodded. "First off, I didn't mean to . . . insult you about the not . . . going there thing. That came out the wrong way."

Unwanted hope sparked in her chest.

"Pretending nothing happened between us within the last twenty-four hours is as stupid as pretending nothing happened three years ago. We can't keep pretending."

Madison's head bobbed.

"And I think it's obvious that I'm attracted to you." His

gaze dipped again, and the bubbles were almost gone. Parts of pink flesh peeped through. "That I want you."

Her breath stilled as her heart galloped. Okay. Wow. This was so unexpected, she had no idea what to say or do.

Chase's eyes were like chips of heated blue ice that melted her as he continued. "You've gotten under my skin, and I've done everything to ignore it, because caving to it . . . it isn't right."

She blinked. "Why? Why isn't it right, Chase?"

He moved to sit down on the edge of the tub, so close to her, his presence swamped her. "It's not what you think, Maddie."

She had no idea what she thought anymore. "Then tell me."

Drawing in a short breath, his gaze moved to where her feet popped out of the water, the nails painted a crimson red. He didn't answer.

Unsure if his lack of response was a good thing or not, she lowered her feet under the water. It was growing colder and she was going to be pickled if she stayed much longer.

He shook his head, that half smile back again. "Wanting what I want from you . . . it's never going to work out. You know my history. You know . . . what I grew up in. And you're Mitch's sister. It's like spitting in his face."

Madison blinked. "You're not your father."

Chase said nothing.

"And . . . Mitch does trust you, but you're not disrespecting him. It has nothing to do with him." Lifting her chin, she met his eyes. "I understand what you're getting at, but . . ."

"But?" His brows rose.

Madison took a deep breath. "But we're consenting adults, Chase. We don't need my brother's permission. And you're your own person."

"It's not just about getting his permission."

It struck her then that Chase needed someone to believe in him, because his hang-up wasn't Mitch, it wasn't even her. And suddenly the comment he made earlier about her being too good made sense.

He honestly thought she was too good for him.

Her heart squeezed. Couldn't he see what everyone else saw, that underneath it all, he was a good guy with standards? Could seeing his father mistreat his mom have warped him to this point, where he believed himself incapable of being in a relationship? Even with her, someone who had known him his whole life? Maybe all he needed was a tiny push over that hang-up. And that push would have to be from her, and it would have to be drastic.

Swallowing, she placed her hands on the cool edge of the ceramic tub and pushed herself up. Water ran in rivulets down her body. Soapy bubbles slid over her thighs. The air was cool against her warm flesh, and she couldn't believe she had done it. Stood completely naked in front of Chase, and if he refused her now, gave her any excuse, she would never be able to come back from that rejection.

Chase's nostrils flared as he leaned back, his hands clenching in his lap. "Jesus Christ . . ."

Feeling exposed, she fought to keep her arms at her sides and let him look his fill. And boy was he ever looking his fill. Everywhere his gaze went, she felt the heated intensity igniting her flesh. Her skin pricked and flamed. Warmth flooded her, pooling in her core.

"Towel?" she said, voice husky.

He stared at her so long she began to wonder if he'd lost the ability to speak. And then she saw it—the moment he cracked wide open, and she was thrilled. "No."

Her pulse pounded. "No?"

Chase placed his hands on her hips. The touch of his skin on hers sent chills over her. She let him help her out of the tub, made no sound as he tugged her between the *V* of his thighs. She waited with her heart in his hands as he leaned forward, pressing a sweet kiss against the flare of her hip.

Madison's chest swelled and heat speared her body as his mouth moved up her flat stomach, his tongue dancing around her navel. She grabbed his shoulders as her head tipped back, and his mouth traveled up . . . and up.

Her body went weak at the first touch of his mouth on her breast, hot and demanding. His lips were soft yet firm, lingering and coaxing tiny moans from her parted lips. Her body turned to liquid under his skilled touch.

"Open your legs for me," he ordered.

Beyond control of her own body, she obeyed and jerked when she felt the first light touch of his hand between her thighs. Chase's fingers were feather light, teasing as he worked her into a state where her hips were moving against his hand, back arching, begging for more. And then he gave her more, slipping a finger inside her and then two.

Panting, she felt her fingers dig through the shirt he wore, into the hard skin of his shoulders as her body rocked. His thumb moved in circles over the bundle of nerves at the juncture of her thighs. Her body coiled deep inside her core, and she felt herself start to splinter, to come apart.

Chase removed his hand, and before she could cry out in denial, he pressed his lips to the inside of her thigh. Her heart stopped and then doubled up erratically. It had been long, so very long, since something this intimate had been done to her.

"I want to taste you," he growled, nuzzling the inside of her thigh. "Tell me you want me to. Please."

"Yes," she moaned, and then nodded, just in case he didn't get the picture, because if he didn't, dear God, she was going to drown him in the bathtub. And wouldn't that be embarrassing to explain to the police and all the family?

He slid to his knees, and the first touch of his mouth nearly broke her. It was a gentle sweep of his lips, a sweet, chaste kiss that started off as a slow boil and then exploded as he deepened the touch, his tongue slipping the length of her and then inside.

Chase burrowed into her flesh, sucking, tugging, and licking until her back bowed and she cried out his name. She was on the verge, hanging over the edge and then her release sped through her, pitching her so high, to a place where only white heat and sensations existed. And he kept going, drinking her in as another climax started and broke apart again, her cries hoarse as her body spasmed.

When she came back down, Chase had sat on the edge of the tub again and was holding her in his lap, his cheek resting on her shoulder. His hands traced an idle, smooth circle along her lower back, following the curve of her spine.

Madison didn't protest when he leaned back, his vibrant blue eyes hooded. Those dimples appeared on his striking face, and she wanted to kiss them. She wanted to do all kinds of things. Starting with repaying him . . .

Madison reached down, wanting to feel his length, but he stopped her. "We still need to talk," he said, his fingers pressing into the flesh of her hips again as he placed her on her feet.

Talk? She didn't think she was capable of forming a coherent sentence. Tiny droplets of water sprayed from her soaked hair when she shook her head.

Chase chuckled as he rose. Reaching around her, he grabbed the towel and slowly, carefully dried her off before wrapping the oversized material around her breasts.

"Now," he said, pressing a kiss to her forehead, "I can concentrate."

She stared up at him, doubting how affected he really was when he could engineer her lust like that and not take any pleasure for himself. Stirrings of unease began in her belly, a not-so-pleasant thing to feel after something so mind-blowingly wonderful. "Well, I can't."

Taking her hand, he led her out of the bathroom to the bed. She sat, clutching the edge of the towel, very unsure of everything again. Especially when his emotions were on lockdown, his face blank, but his eyes . . .

He stood before her, legs spread in a powerful, dominant stance. "I want you."

You have me, she wanted to say. "I think we've established that."

His lips curved at the corners. "And you want me."

"Another known fact," she said. *A well-known fact, that is,* but there was no need for her to point that out. "Where is this conversation going?" Because she wanted to finish it, strip him naked, and finally get him where she'd always wanted him. Oddly, a heart-shaped bed was never in her fantasies, but she was okay with improvising.

"And I care about you. I really do." Chase knelt before her, his eyes meeting hers. "There's only one option."

Hope was back again, beating at her insides like a hyper butterfly. Caring about someone didn't mean loving her, but Chase wasn't the type of man to proclaim his undying devotion, especially with the daddy issues. But she could work with this. And of course, there was only one option. Cut the crap and be together. Face her brother, admit that they cared for each other, and deal with it. Together, she could prove to him that he was nothing like his dad. That he was worth everything. Then they could finally discover if there really was a fairy-tale ending for them. And of course, lots and lots of sex in the near future.

"I agree," she said, fighting a goofy grin that would make her look like she'd been smacked with the idiot branch.

"Good. Great." His shoulders relaxed. "Because this is what we both need."

God, did she ever need this—need him.

Chase smiled. "And once we do it, then . . . things will be normal again. It'll be over."

She started to nod in agreement, because she was still knee deep in her fantasy coming true, but what he said slowly sank in. Icy dread drifted over her skin. "Come again?"

"Having sex," he explained as he rose and leaned forward,

placing his palms on either side of her thighs, caging her in. "We do it. Get it over with. Because obviously we can't go back to things being normal until we do."

That horrible chilled feeling seeped through her skin, leaving her numb. "Being normal?"

"Yeah, like things were before. We can be friends again." He placed a large hand on her shoulder, and she flinched. Chase frowned. "No harm. No foul."

Madison was having a hard time processing what he was saying. How long had she waited to hear him admit that he cared for her, wanted her, and this . . . this was added onto the end, like a disclaimer of doom?

An ache opened up in her chest.

He cupped the nape of her neck, tilting her head back. He placed a kiss under her chin, the gesture so sweet and gentle tears filled her eyes.

Because the gesture really meant nothing.

"Say something, Maddie." He let go, moving back onto his haunches.

She wasn't sure if she *could* say anything. A lump had formed in her throat, and it was quickly moving up. Her insides felt bruised, and when she spoke, her voice was hoarse. "So . . . so that's the magical fix? We have sex to get it out of our systems?"

"I wouldn't call it a magical fix," he said, head cocked to the side. "But it's something, right?"

It was something, all right, and no matter how badly she wanted him, it wasn't enough. And God, did that sting like a bitch? No, it was worse than a sting. It was like being cut wide open.

"Wow," she murmured, somewhat dumbfounded. "That's such a romantic proposition, how could I refuse?"

His lips formed a tight line. "You don't need to be a smartass about it."

She laughed, but it was brittle sound. "How am I supposed to be, Chase?"

Standing straight, he took a step back and shook his head. "Maddie—"

"Let me get this straight," she said, coming to her feet. Her legs shook. Her one free hand trembled as she crossed the distance between them and stopped. "You're worried about disrespecting Mitch by being with me and you don't want to treat me like your dad treated your mom, but somehow, in your head, sleeping with me to get it out of your system is less offensive?"

Chase opened his mouth, but nothing came out. Maybe he realized his mistake, but it didn't matter. It was too late.

Heart breaking into a million stupid little pieces, she smiled tightly. "And even if in some messed-up parallel universe where that would be okay to my brother and you, I wouldn't ever be okay with that."

And then she did something she had never done in her life. Madison smacked him across the cheek.

Chapter Eight

Well, that hadn't gone as planned. Not that Chase really had a plan. Over an hour later, his cheek was still stinging like hell and the bathroom door she had slammed shut in his face was still ringing in his ears.

God, he'd mucked everything up in the worst kind of way.

As he had sat on the couch, wondering how in the hell he could fix this, he'd heard the water running in the bathroom and knew she wasn't showering again. Maddie was too proud.

She'd turned the water on to mask her tears.

Damn it. The last thing Chase wanted to do was hurt her and damn if he hadn't. He felt like the worst kind of son of a bitch.

Finally, she had emerged from the bathroom, eyes puffy but face clear as she stalked past him, dressed in another pretty little dress that matched the green flecks in her eyes, and left the cabin without saying a word, her spine unnaturally stiff.

He'd tried to stop her—he'd gone to the bathroom door several times over—but he'd said nothing, because really, what could he say now? How could he fix this? He should've just kept his damn mouth shut and let it go.

By the time he stood from the couch and changed into a pair of dark slacks and a light dress shirt for the formal dinner, he was already running a few minutes late.

Most everyone had arrived to the dining hall in the main lodge by the time Chase finally trudged in. Mitch and Lissa sat at the head of the table, side by side, holding hands. And then on either side of them were their parents, followed by the . . . God damn, the bridal party.

Maddie sat, one leg primly crossed over the other, hands folded in her lap, and spine still straight. The seat beside her was empty.

The seating was assigned.

Squaring his shoulders, he headed to his seat, nodding in response to various greetings.

Maddie didn't look at him, didn't say a word.

He glanced at her from the corner of his eye. Her jaw was tight, lips pressed into a small line.

Across from him, Chad stood with a glass of wine in his hand. "Now that we're all here, it's time for a toast."

"And hopefully something to eat," Mitch said, grinning. Lissa playfully smacked his arm, and he laughed. "Go ahead, Chad."

Chad cleared his throat melodramatically. Half the table was leaning forward, dying to hear what he was actually going to say. One never knew with him.

"I think we can all agree that no one is surprised to be here," he started out, raising his glass high in the air. "From the moment Mitch and Lissa met, we knew he was whipped."

Laughter followed, and at the head of the table, Mitch shrugged, accepting what was true. Even though the two had started off as friends, it had been obvious that Mitch had the hots for the pretty blonde.

Chase's gaze met his eldest brother's. Chandler quirked an eyebrow and then glanced at Maddie.

"Most of us were taking bets to see how long he went before asking her out." Chad grinned at Lissa's surprised expression. "Yep, I said a week. Chandler called two weeks, and good ole Chase said a month and a half."

Lissa gasped and then grinned. "Mitch asked me out when we'd known each other close to two months." Her wide smile turned on Chase. "You won."

He shrugged as he toyed with the stem of his wineglass. Although a lot of eyes were on him, a lot of smiles, Maddie stared straight ahead.

"Betting aside," Chad went on, "we all knew that Lissa and Mitch were the real deal. No two better people could've met. So cheers!"

Glasses rose and a roar of liveliness filled the room. Chase was surprised his brother had relatively behaved himself during the speech. Then it was his turn, and as the best man, he was honor-bound to humiliate his buddy, but like Chad, he kept it simple: short and sweet.

The food arrived and the dinner progressed as it should, for the most part. Everyone around him was celebrating the union of two people who deserved it, but him? He was thrilled for them, but . . .

Chase glanced at Maddie as she spoke to one of the bridesmaids.

He was an asshole. There was no way around it, and he knew deep down that she was never going to forgive him for his offer. Not that he blamed her. It was tantamount to offering her money for sex. Worse than anything his father did.

Appetite vanished, he pushed his plate back and tried to listen to what one of his college buds was saying. But he noted that Maddie stayed away from the wine. At least there would be no repeat of her dancing with the dickhead.

A possessive feeling surged inside him as he recalled the guy putting his hands on her hips, lifting her off the bench. That guy had no right touching her.

Chase sucked in a sharp breath.

Hell, he had no right to touch her.

When dinner was over, the party broke into small groups and he couldn't help but notice Maddie steered straight toward her brother and family. Pressure built in his chest, like a sudden weight, settling hard.

Knowing he needed to fix things, but not sure if he could, he felt his mood plummet from bad to shit, which wasn't improved when Chad sauntered up to him and dropped a heavy arm over his shoulders.

"Little brother," he said. "You've got that look on your face."

Chase casually shrugged his brother's arm off but took the beer he offered with his other hand. "What look?"

"The same look you had before you knocked the crap out of Rick Summers for getting too friendly with Maddie in the car that one night."

Chase didn't like where this conversation was going.

"It's the same look you got when Maddie was a freshman in college and some guy in your econ class said he wanted to tap that ass."

The muscle in Chase's jaw started to tick. Only Chad knew about that. He'd witnessed it. Recalling the little punk and the horseshit he'd been saying pissed him off all over again.

"And it's the same look you got on your face last night when she was dancing with that guy," Chad went on. He smiled when Chase sent him a look. "Yeah, I noticed. And you've sat through dinner like someone kicked your puppy into traffic, burned down all three of your bars, then pissed in your face and shoved a fat one up—"

Chase laughed dryly. "I get what you're saying."

"You didn't even smile during my toast."

He rolled his eyes.

"And man," Chad said after a moment. "What did you do to Maddie? Because she had the same look on her face the entire time."

"It has nothing to do with Maddie." He downed half his beer. "And I don't want to talk about it."

Chad shook his head and ignored Chase's words. "It's always her."

He went stock still, staring at the bottle of beer. "Is it that obvious?" he asked on a choked breath. He expected Chad to joke with him, but he remained dead silent.

"Yeah, it's that obvious," Chad said finally. "Always has been."

"Great."

Chad smiled then. "So what happened?"

He took another long draft of his beer and then told Chad a brief, not-so-explicit version of what happened. As expected, his brother stared at him like he was the biggest kind of idiot.

"I can't believe you made that offer." Shaking his head, he laughed. "What did you expect? For her to jump right on that?"

Honestly, looking back, Chase wasn't sure what the hell he'd expected. Somewhere between the incident in the wine cellar and seeing her in the bathtub, so absurdly sexy surrounded by bubbles, it had been the best thing he could come up with.

Chase tugged a hand through his hair. "I don't know what I was thinking."

"That's the problem," Chad said. "You were thinking too much."

Chase scowled. "That makes zero sense."

"You don't get it. You're overthinking this whole thing when you should be doing what your heart is telling you."

Chase busted into laughter. "Wow, been watching a lot of *Oprah* reruns?"

"Shut up," Chad said, stretching his arms over his head. Chase could tell he was uncomfortable as hell in the dress clothes. While Chase favored the nicer stuff, Chad was comfortable only in jeans.

His brother flashed a wild grin. "Okay, how about starting to think with what's between your legs? Either way, the Mitch thing is bullshit. You know he wouldn't have a problem with you getting serious about Maddie. Unless you're only interested in hitting it, and hey, I can understand that; she's a fine piece of—"

"Finish that sentence and I'll shove this bottle up your ass," Chase warned.

Chad tipped his head back and laughed. "Yeah, so like I expected, it's not a one-night thing, so I doubt Mitch would have a problem with it."

"Let me ask you a question. If we had a sister, how would you feel if one of our friends was snooping around her skirt?"

"That's a bad example." Chad folded his arms, eyes narrowing on one of the pretty bridesmaids. "Our friends suck."

Chase snorted.

His brother fell silent again, another oddity for Chad. Several seconds passed. "Bro, all of us are a little fucked up."

"No shit."

Chad let out a dry laugh. "What we saw our dad do to our mother was messed up. Father was a dick, dead or alive. But you know what the messed-up thing is? That we're still letting him screw up our lives for us, and he's not even around."

Part of Chase wanted to deny it, but he couldn't lie to his brothers. Of all people, they knew. "I'm just like him."

"You're nothing like him," Chad said heatedly. "But you make yourself like him. I don't even know why. It's like some kind of twisted self-fulfilling prophecy."

"There's that *Oprah* shit again."

"Shut up, asshole. I'm being serious." Chad placed his hand on Chase's shoulder. "Out of all of us, you're the best one and don't even try to deny it. All your life, you've wanted Maddie. She's been the one thing that kept your ass grounded and for whatever reason, you keep pushing her away."

This conversation was starting to go into no-man's-land. Mainly because it was starting to make sense. "Drop it—"

"I'm not finished. Hear me out, bro. You're not Father. You would never treat Maddie like he treated Mom. Hell, those women you date? You even treat them better. If anything, they prove you're not like him."

"What kind of effed-up logic is that?"

Chad shot him a knowing look. "You're not leading on a single one of them. You haven't lied to them. You're not married and flaunting your whores in front of your wife's face."

A sharp pang of fear—of actual fear—hit him in the gut. What if he did do that? He could never forgive himself. "I'm not married. That could be the reason."

"You'd never do that to Maddie," his brother said. "You know why?"

"I bet you're going to tell me."

Chad took a long swig of his beer, finishing it off. "Because you have something that Father never had—the capacity to love. And you love Maddie too much to do that to her."

Chase opened his mouth to deny it, but damn if the words weren't there.

His brother started to back away, brows raised. "You aren't going to taint her, bro. You aren't going to screw her up. I think the problem here is that you're not giving anyone credit, especially yourself."

Madison had seriously considered camping out on the floor of her parents' cabin, but the whole second-honeymoon thing just grossed her out. Most of the wedding party was paired up with the exception of Sasha, who was Lissa's friend from Maryland, but it looked like she'd be entertaining Chad for the evening.

That left her great aunt Bertha, and yeah, that was so not happening.

Besides, she told herself as she entered the dark, empty cabin, *I'm not a teenager anymore.* She wouldn't run from Chase. It didn't matter that once again she had held her heart in her hands and he'd taken it, dropped it on the floor, and stomped on it. All she needed to do was make it through tonight and tomorrow, and then for the rest of the weekend, she'd have her own cabin.

She changed quickly, grabbing the shirt Chase had dressed her in last night. A pang hit her in the chest when she remembered how sweet he'd been.

Sweet and sexy, and it meant nothing.

All he wanted was to have sex with her and get it out of his system.

What a douche.

Her hands trembled as she reached for the faucets. Sitting next to Chase for most of the night had been a practice in pure torture. Several times she wanted to turn and say something to him—anything. Or take her glass of water and throw it in his face. The latter would've made her feel better, at least for a few moments.

But there was nothing to be said, and after this weekend, she would go back to her life and finally forget about Chase Gamble.

Washing her face, she tugged her long hair into a ponytail

and went to the bed, settling under the covers. Tonight she didn't feel bad about him ending up on the couch rejected from the sixties. Served him right.

Madison rolled onto her side, placing her back to the door, and squeezed her eyes shut. Mentally tallying up the e-mails she'd need to answer and phone calls to be made when she returned to work next week, she tried to bore herself into sleep before Chase returned.

No such luck.

When the moon was high, its pale light slicing through the wooden shutters, the door creaked open and his footsteps broke the silence.

"Maddie?"

Holding her breath, she pretended to be asleep. *Way to act like a grown-up.*

The footsteps drew closer and then the bed dipped under his weight as he sat. Silence stretched out, taut and tense as her nerves. What was he doing? She was half afraid to find out.

Chase's heavy sigh overshadowed the pounding of her heart. A second later, she felt the very tips of his fingers brush back the strands of hair lying against her cheek, tucking them behind her ear.

"I'm sorry," he whispered, but she heard him. "I'm sorry for everything."

Her breath caught, reminding her that she had indeed been breathing. Madison wasn't sure what his apology should mean. Should it undo everything? Should it just lay between them, a proverbial white flag so there was some hope for a friendship in the future, because there wasn't a future without him, no matter what?

And she wasn't sure who was to blame the most for this catastrophe. Sure, Chase wasn't innocent, but it was she—and the feelings that she'd brought into this—that complicated everything.

Madison squeezed her eyes against the rush of tears and clamped her mouth shut.

Chase hovered for a few more seconds and then the bed shifted as he moved to stand. Unable to stay quiet, to pretend that this wasn't happening, she rolled onto her back. "Chase?"

He froze, one hand planted deep in the covers beside her hip. In the darkness, his eyes looked black, his features stark, strangely open and vulnerable.

She really didn't know what she was doing. Her body was at war with her heart and thoughts, and ever since she was a child, she'd had terrible, horrific impulse control.

She reached up, placing her hand on his smooth jaw. Instead of pulling away, he pressed his cheek into her hand and closed his eyes.

"This has been a wedding to remember, huh?" he said, his cheek rising against her hand as he gave a little smile. "And there hasn't even been a wedding yet."

Then he placed his hand over hers and slowly brought it to his lips. He pressed a kiss to her palm, and her heart flipped over. "I'm sorry, Maddie. I really am. I don't know what the hell I was thinking to say that to you earlier. Getting it out of my system isn't what I want."

Her fingers curled around his. Confusion swept through her. "I don't . . . I don't understand."

He drew in a deep breath. "I don't even know what I'm

thinking. Chad was spouting all this *Oprah* bullshit and some of it made sense—as insane as that is."

"What?"

Chase smiled a little, and then his eyes met hers. "I want you."

Madison's breath caught. Hope was back, beating at her insides. With Chase, everything was like a roller coaster. Up. Down. Up. Down. "You said that earlier."

"And I meant it."

So much confusion still churned inside her, but her heart moved on, creating more space for him. The word that left her mouth pretty much sealed her fate. "Stay?"

Chase hesitated, his body going so still, so tense that she could feel the edginess rolling off of him. Then he sprang into motion, kicking off his shoes as he unbuttoned his shirt. It fluttered to the floor like a white flag.

Her heart was in her throat as her gaze flickered over the expanse of his well-defined chest, across the dips of his rock-hard abs. He was beautiful, something straight out of her fantasies. In the pale light of the moon, in the shadows of the cabin, she swept aside her reservations and fear. She existed on what she always had—her love for Chase.

And in an instant, she believed this was the turning point that had been building for years. There'd be no going back. And if she couldn't prove that he wasn't like his father, no one could.

Chase shifted onto his side, facing her with very little space between them. Neither of them said anything as she twisted toward him, their faces and bodies inches apart.

Slowly, tentatively, Chase placed his hand to her cheek.

His fingers trailing along the arch of her face, down to her parted lips. She felt the light touch in every cell of her body and her response was immediate, consuming.

His fingers drifted down her throat, to the edge of her cotton shirt. A small smile played across his lips. "Do you know that seeing you in my clothes is a huge turn-on?" He edged his fingers under the collar, brushing them across her collarbone, and her toes curled. "I don't know why that is, but it is."

She wondered if he felt the same when she was out of his clothes. Then she remembered the hard length that had pressed against her in the bathroom and she went with a yes.

"What do we do, Maddie?" he asked, voice deep and husky.

Madison swallowed, her body joining her heart and already making up her mind for her. Before she even knew what she was doing, her body moved toward his.

Rising up on her knees, she placed both hands on his shoulders and pushed him until he was flat on his back. She straddled his hips, biting back a moan when she felt his erection straining through the rich material of his trousers, hot against the *V* of her thighs.

"Make love to me," she whispered. "Please."

Chase stilled and then his thick lashes lifted, his stare piercing her. He didn't answer, but he placed his hands on her thighs, sliding them up to the hem of the shirt. His fingers bunched the material. There was a pause, a moment when the only thing moving was her pounding heart, and then he lifted the shirt up.

And that was her answer.

By the time the borrowed shirt joined his on the floor, her mouth was on his and his big, warm body was under hers. The kiss wasn't soft or gentle. It was deep and scorching, a product of years of pent-up desire on both their sides. His lips swallowed her breathy moans as his hand landed on the small of her back and jerked her to his chest. The feel of his skin flush with hers swamped her senses. Chase kissed her like a man starved, possessed by need . . . need for her. Madison's hands clutched his shoulders as he staked his claim.

A hand tangled in her hair. "If we're going to stop," he whispered against her swollen lips, "we need to stop now. Do you understand me?"

She shuddered as his teeth nipped at her bottom lip. "I don't want to stop. Ever. Do you understand me?"

He stilled again, and then with a near-feral growl, he moved so quickly that in a heartbeat, she was on her back, open and vulnerable to him, and he hovered above her. Concentration marked his striking features, emphasizing his full lips.

Then he was on her. His mouth clamping down on the tip of her breast as he hastily worked on the buttons and fly of his trousers. Madison let out a strangled cry as her back bowed off the mattress.

Flesh against flesh, she felt him hot and hard against her thigh, and she gripped his arms, placing tiny kisses all over his face and down his throat.

Chase caught Madison's chin, held her as his mouth plundered hers again, kissing her until she writhed and thrashed beneath him. He was in control. Part of her wouldn't have wanted it any other way.

Some reality snuck back in, and she placed a hand on his chest. "I'm on the pill, but . . ."

A wry smile tugged on his lips. "I got it covered." He was off her, rummaging around in his luggage for a few moments before he returned with a foil package in his hand.

Madison arched a brow. "Planning to get laid this weekend?"

"Not really," he admitted. "But I always have some with me."

There wasn't any time to let jealousy seep in because her gaze dropped and her stomach hollowed as she watched him slide the condom on his thick shaft. Then his lips were on hers and he was guiding her back, stretching out over her.

Amazed by the power in his body, she ran her hands down his ripped stomach and around his taut hips. His skin was like satin stretched over steel. Perfect.

The taste of him was on her lips as the kisses slowed, turned tender as she felt him hot at her entrance. Rolling her hips, she moaned at the feel of him there, close but not close enough. She was so ready, had been ready for what felt like an eternity.

Rising up on his elbows, Chase stared down at her. His eyes were a heated, vibrant sapphire, penetrating and intense as they locked onto hers.

"Don't stop," she whispered. "I want to feel you inside me."

"I couldn't stop now, even if I wanted." He kissed her, marking her with all the passion and yearning she had felt for so long. "I need this. Damn it, I need you."

And then he plunged into her with one deep stroke.

Madison let out a keening cry at the feel of him stretching and filling her. None of her fantasies, none of the men she had been with in the past, had ever felt like this, because this . . . this was completion.

He stilled, seated deep inside her. One hand came up, brushing the damp hair back from her forehead. "You're so tight . . ." His voice was guttural, near animalistic. "Are you okay?"

She nodded and then wrapped her legs around his hips. Chase tipped his head back, groaning, and then she rocked her hips up. The veins in his neck protruded, as they did in his arms. And then he started to move, slow and languid strokes that drove her crazy. The friction of their bodies moving together, the sounds in the otherwise silent cabin, heightened her pleasure.

Lost . . . Madison was lost.

For so long, he held back while she cried out for more, and when he finally gave it to her, she gasped as his hands clamped down on her wrists, holding her still. He thrust hard, her hips surging to meet his.

Pressure built inside her, zinging through her veins like bottled lightning. It was too much—too intense. Her head kicked back, her body trembling.

"Come for me," Chase whispered against her neck. "Let go."

And Madison did. She came apart, shattering around him as she called out his name. Two quick, hard thrusts later and she felt him find his release, his huge body spasming over hers as aftershocks racked his body.

When it was over, he eased out of her and onto his back,

gathering her close so that her cheek rested above his pounding heart. Both of them struggled with their breathing.

She'd never felt anything like that before and knew she'd never feel it again. Heaven.

Madison closed her eyes. There was a good chance she'd regret this in the harsh light of the morning and after weeks, maybe months from now. But in a few years, she'd be able to look back and know that she'd had him, if only for one night.

Chapter Nine

Lazily, Madison stretched and smiled at the pleasant burn in her muscles. Last night . . . yes, it had probably been the best night of her life. No lie. After Chase had a few moments to recover, he'd flipped her onto her stomach, drew up to her knees and . . . yeah, like she said, best night of her life. And her body was already warming, readying for him again.

Last night had to have been a turning point for them. The way he'd . . . the way he'd made love to her, it meant something deep, irrevocable, and perfect. She just knew it. Somehow they'd burned down those barriers without words. He had to see he was so much better than his father and he had to know that they were meant for this.

She rolled over and reached for the warmth of his body and found . . . nothing.

Her eyes snapped open.

The spot next to her was empty, but the scent of woods and something wild lingered on the pillow and twisted sheets.

Madison turned to the couch, but that, too, was empty. A deep sense of foreboding took root, and she scrambled off the bed, clutching a sheet around her. She checked the bathroom, but he wasn't there, either.

He'd left without saying anything.

Her heart turned over painfully.

Okay. She was being stupid. He could be doing anything. Getting them breakfast or walking outside, enjoying the clean morning air.

Hurrying over to the window, she parted the blinds, wincing at the bright glare. The deck was empty. As far as she could see, there was no Chase. Turning around, she shivered as her gaze drifted over the bed. He didn't leave her, not after a night like that. There was no way, because that . . . that would be like working it out of your system. That would be like getting what you wanted and then bailing, like guys did on one-night stands.

Last night wasn't a one-night stand.

Her gaze traveled to the couch again, then to where her suitcase was near the small closet, and then . . . her eyes darted back to the suitcase.

Coldness seeped into her bones.

His luggage was gone.

Heart pounding, she crossed the room and threw open the closet door. Two of her dresses and her bridesmaid's dress hung in the closet, but all of Chase's stuff—his tux, his dress shirts—was gone. As were his shoes, and she knew if she checked the bathroom, his stuff would be gone from there, too.

Madison stood in front of the closet until she realized she was shaking.

He'd left her.

He'd actually left her.

In a numb, painful daze, she went back to the bed and sat on the edge. Her throat burned and her eyes stung, but she clamped it down, pushed it all down. Minutes turned into an hour and still he didn't show.

He really had left her.

Her brain had a hard time processing it, but the evidence was clear. She was a fool. Last night she had given in to her body and her heart, and it had come back and bit her in the ass.

Maybe she should've listened to him. He's warned her— had been warning her all along. He said he was like his father, and he'd proven it.

And he'd demolished her.

Chase wanted to strangle the clerk by the time the man had handed over the key to one of the new cabins. He had made Chase wait for damn near a half an hour while the cabin was cleaned, which put him seriously behind schedule.

Taking his stuff to the new cabin, his eyes gazed at the regular king-size bed with satin sheets. Sheets he could easily see Maddie spread naked upon. That made him think of last night and his cock hardened. He was ready for round three . . . and then round four.

But he needed to shower first. Although he loved the lingering scent of vanilla—of Maddie—the last thing he needed to be doing was running around smelling like he'd just had sex with Mitch's little sister.

Last night had been amazing—Maddie had been amazing. And it was more than sex. It was that connection, that whatever-it-was that went beyond an orgasm. It was something more—special. Once in a lifetime kind of shit. None of the women he'd been with had felt like that, and in that moment, he knew none of them would.

Now *he* sounded like he'd been watching *Oprah* reruns.

But . . . but it had to mean something. And he was tired of fighting the need to find out what that "something" was. Tired of denying what he really wanted—had wanted for far too long. Maddie was more than Mitch's little sister. More than the little girl who'd shadowed him for years. She was everything to him. And he was more than his father's son, too, because he knew deep down he could never hurt Maddie. Not after last night.

And now he was just realizing that?

He'd mucked up things yesterday with that God-awful offer, but last night . . .

It had to be a new beginning.

He took the fastest shower of his life and then headed back to the lodge. There was a tiny florist shop in the back, and he picked up a dozen roses. Tucking them under one arm, he grabbed a slice of cheesecake from the in-house bakery before making his way back to the Love Shack.

Chase was hoping Maddie was still asleep. He had a real good idea of how to wake her, with his hands, fingers, and then his tongue. Maybe some cheesecake afterward, but knowing her, she'd probably knock him over to get to the good stuff. No one got between Maddie and the sweets.

He climbed out of his car stiffly and strolled into the cabin. His gaze went straight to the bed—the empty bed.

"Maddie?"

The cabin was unnaturally quiet. No shower was running. Nothing. Putting the roses and slice of cheesecake down on the end table, his gaze danced around the room. "Shit."

Maddie was gone. So was her large suitcase. Peering into the bathroom, he found no trace of her. Her blow dryer and curling iron were gone, as if she'd never been there.

Cursing under his breath again, he spun around and stalked to the front door. He was going to find her, drag her back here . . . With his hand on the door, he stopped.

Two problems: He had no idea where Maddie went. She couldn't have gone far, but she could be in any number of cabins, and short of banging like holy hell on every door, he needed a better game plan. And two, he didn't know why she'd left. After last night, it seemed pretty obvious what he wanted, so he couldn't even fathom why she'd leave, especially when he'd already gotten another cabin for them, one not outfitted with a heart-shaped bed and velveteen blankets.

Though, he was going to kind of miss that bed.

Chase drew back from the door, thrusting his hands through his hair. A game plan for what? Chasing after Maddie? Shit. How the tables had turned.

He spun around, his gaze falling to the rumpled sheets on that damn bed.

Double shit.

Scrubbing the palms of his hands down his face, he then snatched the flowers up and left the cheesecake behind. The first place he went by was her parents' cabin. They were sitting on the deck, enjoying tea while thumbing through a wilderness survival magazine. Chase shook his head as he fought a grin. The two of them looked like a normal couple on the verge of retirement.

Maddie's father looked up first, smiling broadly. "Hey, Chase, what are you up to?"

"Nothing much," he said, leaning against the railing. "Hello, Mrs. Daniels."

She smiled, shaking her head. "Honey, it's about time you start calling me Megan. And those flowers! Aren't they lovely?" Her eyes glimmered. "May I ask who they're for?"

"A lovely person," he replied.

"Is that so . . ."

Mr. Daniels was on his feet, bringing the magazine over to him. "I'm glad you swung by. You can help end a debate between me and the wifey here."

A picture of a man in a flannel jacket standing next to a herd of cows was shoved in his face before he could respond. "Organic beef," Maddie's father announced. "I'm trying to tell Megan here that even if an apocalypse happens, most people will still want some meat on their plates."

So accustomed to these types of questions, Chase took it in good stride. "I'm sure people will still want a steak."

"Exactly!" Mr. Daniels agreed. "So I said we should 'sponsor' a herd of cattle and put them up for sale. The lovely wife over there thinks it's a waste of time."

"And money," Mrs. Daniels added, twisting in her seat to face the two men. "I'm pretty sure the last thing people will be thinking about during nuclear fallout is a medium-rare steak."

Chase smiled. "Or a zombie apocalypse."

Mrs. Daniels threw up her hands. "That's what I've been saying."

Her husband huffed. "When the sun doesn't shine for three years and you've run out of mint leaves to eat, you'll want a steak."

She rolled her eyes. "That would be the last of our worries."

"Wait." Chase stepped in. "How would you be keeping the cows alive if the sun isn't shining?"

Mr. Daniels straightened. "Underground bunkers large enough to hold organically grown fields. There are bunkers all over the world, bigger than five or so football field lengths. Like Noah's Ark—"

"Chase doesn't care about Noah's Ark, so before you get started on that, we're not going to start selling Build-Your-Own-Arks, either." She smiled at Chase. "You couldn't imagine the cost of warehousing something like that."

"No, ma'am," Chase said, grinning.

Mr. Daniels snapped the magazine shut. "This discussion isn't over."

Sighing, his wife shook her head. "Are you looking for Madison, dear?"

Taken aback, Chase wondered if it was that obvious. "Well, actually, I was."

Mr. Daniels returned to the table, smacking the magazine down. "You lose your roommate?"

"Seems that way," Chase said.

"We haven't seen her, dear, but you might what to check with Lissa." Mrs. Daniels took a sip of tea. "They're probably getting things ready for tomorrow."

Thanking both of them, he started up the pathway. If Maddie was with Lissa, he didn't want to bother her, but . . .

Chase found himself at the front desk of the lounge. The clerk stared back at him, clearly not wanting to go for round two already. "Was the new cabin you gave me this morning the only one available?" Chase asked.

Bob inclined his head, as if confused. "No. There were two. Both were readied this morning." He started pecking away at his computer. "Was the one we assigned this morning unsuitable?"

He took a deep breath. "No. It's perfect. What about the other room?"

"For Miss Daniels?" he asked, smiling fondly. Obviously Maddie had left a much better impression on the clerk than he had. "She stopped by maybe twenty minutes ago and picked up the key for cabin six."

Chase stared at the clerk, feeling as if he'd been punched in the stomach. Anger lit off a firestorm inside him. As irrational as it was, he was pissed and offended. She left him after last night?

Spinning around, he left the clerk without a second glance, tossing the roses in the trash on the way out.

Madison was in a weird state of mind. Caught between the remnants of absolute bliss she'd experienced last night and the coldness that had lingered deep inside since she'd left the cabin, she wasn't sure if she should feel happy or sad.

Mostly sad, she decided as she stuffed little white bells into the boxes being used for wedding keepsakes. At least she'd had a night to experience. No more wondering what it would be like to be with Chase. Now she knew. It was amazing.

Her heart ached.

That afternoon she'd almost called Bridget again, but she figured that conversation was best to have in person. No way would she want to miss all of Bridget's what-the-hell expressions when she described how she basically straddled Chase and he'd bailed on her the next morning.

Madison glanced up as one of the bridesmaids dumped a truckload of mints in front of them. She snatched one, starving, since she'd been too wired this morning to eat.

Lissa giggled. "Are they any good?"

Popping one in her mouth, Madison nodded. "Minty. Very yummy."

"Speaking about yummy," Sasha, a bridesmaid, said. "I think the Gamble brothers' nickname should be yummy."

Cindy, another bridesmaid, snorted as she glanced at the tall, curvy blonde. "Weren't you all over one of the brothers last night?"

Sasha smiled secretively. "Maybe . . ."

Good to know Madison wasn't the only one. She dropped a bell into a box.

"I can never tell them apart." Cindy grinned.

"They're really easy to tell apart," Madison replied sharply. "They're not triplets."

"Yeah, but the three of them are sex on a stick—dark haired, beautiful blue eyes, and muscles I'd eat chocolate off of," Cindy said, passing one of the other bridesmaids a wicked look. "Of course, if only I wasn't married. Anyway, which one was it? Chase? Chad?"

Madison's eyes narrowed.

"Chad," Sasha answered, her cheeks flushing. "Though,

I wouldn't mind if it had been Chase, too. Hell, all of them at the same time."

The bridesmaids laughed, but Lissa cut Madison a worried look. It probably had something to do with the expression on her face. One that said she was mentally going over how many little metal bells she could shove in Sasha's mouth.

"Didn't you grow up with them, Madison?" Sasha continued, oblivious of the death's door she was knocking on. "Always at your house and stuff? God, I wouldn't have been able to control myself, but I'm sure it's different for you."

Madison shoved a bell through the bottom of the box. "Why is that?"

"Well, I'm sure you're like a little sister to them," she explained. "I mean, aren't you rooming with Chase?"

Crimson swept across her cheeks. Jesus, was that what everyone thought? She had half a mind to go into great detail about just how un-brotherly things were last night with Chase.

"Actually, I'm not sure if that's the case," Lissa said, smiling evenly. "Madison is close to all of them, but from what I've seen . . ." She trailed off, sending Madison a sly look.

Sasha arched an elegant brow. "Well, then, kudos to you . . ."

After that, the girls pretty much kept mum about the Gamble brothers and Madison, although they did hammer Sasha for juicy details.

Once the boxes were made, the group broke apart to get ready for the rehearsal. Maddie gave Lissa a quick hug and headed back to her new cabin.

She should be happy with her own space, but it was lonely and quiet. And when she took a bath, there was no hope of a surprise visit from Chase.

Sinking deep into the tub, she closed her eyes and tried to push him away. Except Chase was consuming her thoughts on a whole new level, because now she knew what his passion felt like, how he tasted, how he felt inside her.

There was no getting that out of her system.

When she'd woken up this morning, she had been deliciously sore in areas she'd forgotten about and Chase . . . Chase had been gone.

She blew out a long breath and opened her eyes.

Leaving that gaudy cabin had been one of the hardest things she'd ever done. Part of her was still there, but her decision to leave had been simple. However, the decision she had to make going forward would be the hardest she'd ever made and she knew would shock everyone.

"Oh, I can't believe this is happening." Madison's mom grabbed Mitch one more time, blinking back tears. Mrs. Daniels had been dealing out hugs the moment the rehearsal dinner began and there was no end in sight. "My little boy is all grown up."

Mitch winced. "Mom . . ."

She pulled him back to her breast, squeezing and swaying.

Smothering a grin, Madison glanced away and her eyes met her father's. He winked and clamped a hand on her shoulder. "What do you think she'll do when you get married?"

Madison blanched. "Yikes."

Her mom shot her a dirty look over her shoulder, and then she finally released her son and turned to a beaming Lissa. "I know you'll treat my boy right, so I'm going to apologize ahead of time for the waterworks that will ensue starting tomorrow."

"Tomorrow?" grumbled Mr. Daniels. "How about since he announced his intent to marry?"

"Shush it," her mother said, but she grinned.

Madison tucked a loose strand of hair behind her ear as everyone started to move into groups. They'd go through the bridal march, a rundown of the vows, and then it was off to dinner. Then tomorrow . . . tomorrow her brother would get married.

She went up to him with a watery smile. "I'm so happy for you. You're going to make a great husband."

Mitch pulled her into his arms. "Thanks, sis."

"And father," she teased lightly.

He let go, eyes wide. "Dear God, don't say that yet. I want at least a couple of years without a baby Mitch running around."

"Or a baby Lissa."

"Ah, a girl? I don't know if I could deal with that." He shook his head. "It was bad enough fighting off the boys after you."

Madison rolled her eyes. "It was nothing like that."

"Whatever." He dropped his arm over her shoulders. "So, when are you going to settle down? Make Mom's and Dad's lives complete?"

Before she could answer, in strode the Gamble brothers. Chad and Chandler flanked Chase, who was dressed in a pair of dark trousers and a loose-fitting buttoned shirt. Strands of damp hair curled around his ears. The tips of his cheekbones were slightly flushed and his eyes were a steely blue.

He looked absolutely stunning.

Madison hoped her brother didn't notice how she stiffened, but of course, luck had never really been on her side.

Mitch chuckled, but she elbowed him in the stomach and escaped before the herd of brothers could descend on them. She made a beeline for Lissa and the other bridesmaids. Avoiding Chase completely would be out of the question, but as long as they didn't have any real amount of time alone together, she could do this without breaking down.

Or getting her heart trampled on even more. And there was only one way to do that. It hurt like hell; it killed a little part of her—the one that still believed in fairy-tale endings—but she had no other choice.

Chapter Ten

Avoiding Chase had been successful through most of the rehearsal. Up until they lined up for the bridal procession. She hadn't been alone with him yet, but there was no escaping him now.

Madison fidgeted with a strand of her hair, desperately going for the unaffected look, but Chase's presence beside her was like standing next to the sun, too hot not to feel and too powerful not to look upon.

Staring straight ahead, she pretended to be engrossed in what Sasha was saying to Chad. It had something to do with safe words, and she really wished she hadn't heard any of that. The funny thing about Chad and Chandler was how she did see them as brothers of sorts. Hearing that kind of stuff made her want to gag, but Chase was different. He'd always been different.

"We need to talk," Chase said quietly.

She feigned innocence. "About what?"

His brows slammed down, and she knew right then that he saw through her. He knew her too well. "You know exactly what."

Madison didn't really want to get into the why behind the

reason he left her this morning, moved out of the cabin before she even opened her eyes. And if he offered an apology for last night, she would hit him. Seriously.

Crossing her arms, she refocused on the back of Sasha's platinum hair. "There's nothing to talk about."

"Bullshit."

At the sound of Chase's growl, Sasha glanced over her shoulder, brows arched, but Madison pretended she hadn't heard anything.

Chase shifted closer, lowering his head as his fingers cupped her elbow. She jumped at the unexpected jolt that sent heat zinging through her veins. Against her will, her eyes found his, and she caught his smug grin.

"That's what I thought," he said.

She didn't move, couldn't or just plain wouldn't. "Thought what?"

When he spoke, his voice was a whisper against her cheek. "You're pretending like nothing happened, that you're unaffected, but I know better."

Madison bristled and shot him a glare. "Excuse me?"

"Oh, don't pretend now. You've been hiding from me all day like a little coward—"

"A coward? God. You—"

Up ahead, the wedding planner cleared her throat, interrupting what would have been an epic tirade. "All right, we are going to run through the bridal party," the planner said, voice clipped and as professional as her tight ponytail and crisp pants suit. "At the start of 'Canon in D,' the first couple will lead off and I will give a signal to each additional couple."

Couple? Madison jerked her arm free.

Chase smirked.

The classic instrumental music keyed up, and the first of the procession started forward, arm in arm.

Madison fixed an icy glare on Chase. "You're an arrogant ass," she finished. "I'm not caught up in you as much as you think I am."

"Says the girl who smacked me yesterday and then screamed my name as—"

"Shut up," she hissed, cheeks flushing,

Sasha and Chad went next. The bridesmaid was clinging onto Chad's arm as if she feared he was about to run off. Smart move.

Chase offered his arm. "M'lady?"

Rolling her eyes, she debated ignoring him, but that would draw unnecessary and unwanted attention. Several pairs of eyes were already on them. So, okay, more attention.

Begrudgingly, she placed her arm in the crook of his. "We're not going to talk about last night. It is what it is."

He stared. "You make no sense."

"And I drive you crazy. I get it."

"Miss Daniels and Mr. Gamble," the planner called.

Together, they started forward stiffly. It had to be obvious to everyone present that something was going on between them. Chase looked like he wanted to strangle her, and she had the wide-eyed, deer-in-headlights look. When they reached the end of the aisle, they parted ways. Taking her spot beside Sasha, she glanced over at the groomsmen.

Chase watched her with an intensity that both unnerved and kindled excitement inside her. Betrayed by her heart and now her body, she forced herself to look away. Confusion swept through her like a cold splash of water. Chase didn't understand her? Well, they were two peas in a pod, then, because he'd made it clear yesterday he'd only been interested in a one-night stand. And he'd gotten it.

Unease replaced the confusion rising in her like wisps of acrid smoke.

After Lissa made her entrance, the practice run went smoothly and quickly. Dinner was being set up in the nearest dining hall, and although she was hungry, her stomach roiled. The air became stale in the lodge, and she felt as if she couldn't get a breath.

Excusing herself, she hurried out of the reception hall and toward the back of the lodge. On the deck, she dragged in the fresh, sweetly scented air. She placed her hands on the railing and squeezed until her knuckles ached.

Before the rehearsal, she'd gone to the edge of the property and made a call that had nearly killed her. Her question had been met with shock and a promise to meet up and discuss a few days after she returned home. Hating what she had put into motion, but knowing there was no other option, she blinked back hot tears. It was the first step in the right direction—one that didn't include Chase Gamble in her future.

Chase was frustrated, confused, and a whole lot of pissed off as he stared at Maddie's retreating back. Off and on throughout the years, he and Maddie'd had their spats. Usually over some lame-ass guy she was dating, and after the night in his club, they'd had moments of awkwardness, but this? Never had it been like this.

His hands opened and closed at his sides. Part of him—a huge part—wanted to go to her, pull her into his arms, and kiss the common sense back into her, but the other part was wary of all of this, of Maddie. He just couldn't figure it out. What the hell had he done wrong that had her so spitting mad at him?

Ever since he discovered her gone that morning and settled in to a new cabin, he wanted nothing more than to go to her. What he was going to do with her once he got her he wasn't sure, but he was off-kilter and out of his element in this.

His heart thundered in his chest as he crossed the distance between them. Propping his hip against the railing, he folded his arms. "Why are you hiding from me?"

Those beautiful eyes were closed to him, her lips pinched. "Chase, do we . . . do we really need to do this?"

"What do you think?" He paused. "This isn't like you."

She drew in a breath and it sounded sharp to him. Her lashes swept up and he saw that her eyes were glassy. There was that punch-to-his-stomach feeling. "I'm sorry for being such a bitch in there, but I haven't eaten anything all day, and I think I get moody when I'm low on sugar or something."

"Maddie, I—"

"But we do need to talk about what happened last night." She smiled, but it seemed forced and ugly on her lips. "You were right."

For a moment, shock and surprise held him. "I was?"

"Yes. Last night needed to happen."

Okay, maybe this conversation was going to be better

than he realized. Chase started to relax, but she went on, and damn if it didn't feel like the world was pulled right out from under his feet.

"We needed to get this—whatever it is—out of our systems," she said, her gaze drifting beyond him to where the setting sun cast an orangey glow over the grape trees. "And we did. Things are normal now, right? We're still friends. And we can move on. That's what you wanted—what I want."

Taken aback, he unfolded his arms slowly. That age-old saying filled his head. *Be careful what you wish for* . . . But it wasn't what he wished for. He had no intentions of getting what he wanted and moving on. Better yet, what the hell was happening? What did she think?

"What are you guys doing out here?" Mitch called from the door. "Everyone is waiting for you two to start eating, and you know how Dad gets. He's about to eat the tablecloth."

Blinking rapidly, Maddie laughed as she twisted toward her brother. "We were just watching the sunset, but we're heading in now."

Stunned, Chase watched her walk up to her brother, hugging him tightly before she disappeared back into the lodge. He stood there, incapable of moving or even processing what had just happened. Why was he so shocked? It was what he'd offered—what he'd initially wanted . . . *initially* being the key word.

Fuck. That was all he could think.

"You doing okay, man?" Mitch asked, striding away from the door. He stopped in front of Chase, eyes narrowed. "You're not looking too good."

Chase blinked. "Yeah, I'm . . . I'm fine."

"You sure?" Mitch's gaze turned shrewd. "You're looking a lot like Madison has been."

Chase stiffened. Denials formed on the tip of his tongue but nothing came out.

Several moments passed and then Mitch cracked a half smile. "Look, I hate seeing you like this. You've always been there for me growing up. Remember when Jimmy Decker stole my bike?"

Chase laughed at the unexpected memory. "Yeah, I do."

Mitch grinned. "You stole it back but replaced it with one that had the hand brakes cut. When Jimmy went down the hill . . ." He trailed off with a laugh. "You're the kind of friend who would—"

"Help bury the body, I know." He laughed. "By the way, that brake cutting was really Chad's idea."

"Doesn't surprise me, but seriously, man, you're a good dude. I don't know what's really going on between you and my sister—and don't tell me nothing is, because I have eyes and I know both of you."

Well, damn . . .

"And I don't know what you're thinking," Mitch continued. "I'm not sure I want to, but you're a good guy, Chase. And my sister has always been in love with you."

Chase's gut clenched. *My sister has always been in love with you.* Right up until a few seconds ago when she explained last night had meant nothing more than scratching an itch. Just like he'd suggested in the first place . . . He thought of the roses wilting in the trashcan. Fuck. How he'd planned to christen that updated cabin . . .

He cleared his throat, surprised to find his voice so hoarse. "Nothing . . . nothing is going on with us."

"Bull," Mitch said. "I don't have any problems with you going after her. So if you are waiting on my permission, then you have it as long as you do right by her." His eyes met Chase's. "You get what I'm saying?"

"I do." Chase's voice cracked.

Mitch clasped him on the shoulder. "Now, come on. It's time to eat, celebrate, be merry, and all that shit."

He felt his head nod, but he'd gone numb, completely cold. The irony of everything was a giant F-U. The obstacles that had always held him back from claiming what he wanted were now removed, and it meant nothing.

Pain that felt so very real sliced him in the chest. He took a breath, but it felt like he wasn't breathing at all. His legs were moving, but he wasn't feeling them.

Be careful what you wish for . . .

He should've, because he got it, and it settled in his stomach like a ten-pound weight.

Chapter Eleven

Lissa looked absolutely stunning in her wedding gown. Strapless with a heart-shaped bodice, it was corseted around the waist and slim through the hips, and it floated around her legs like a spring rose blossoming. A fine layer of pearls had been added to the delicate chiffon overlay.

It was a beautiful dress for a beautiful woman, and if Madison ever got married one day, she wanted a dress like this: fresh but also classic.

Madison straightened the last pearl in Lissa's hair and smiled. "You look amazing."

"Thank you." Lissa hugged her and then cast a fond look at their mothers. Both of them were clutching tissues like they were going out of style. "Do you think they'll make it through this?"

"I hope so." Madison grinned, stepping back so that Lissa had a few moments with one of the bridesmaids.

Retreating to the window in the room off from the reception hall, she watched the guests file up the pathway. Outside, Chad and Chandler hovered with a couple of friends from college.

Chase was nowhere to be seen.

Since she had said what needed to be said, he'd kept his distance from her. Which was what she had wanted, but her chest ached, and she was still so very hungry to just be around him.

When Chase had come in after she'd left him on the deck, he had said nothing to her. Didn't even try to approach her once, and after the rehearsal dinner, he'd disappeared with his brother. Obviously he had heard what he needed to and now could rest assured. They were still friends. Everything was normal. The night of passion they shared was already a thing of the past. It was over.

Well, it would be over when she met with her superintendent.

Shaking herself out of her thoughts, she focused on what was going on around her. Mitch and Lissa deserved for her to be here with them, fully here and not just a shell of herself sulking over her own love life.

When it came time to prepare for the bridal march, she was nervous for Lissa and her brother, anxious over seeing Chase, and praying she didn't trip on the hem of her dress.

Out in the hallway, she spotted his broad shoulders. Taking a deep, fortifying breath, she manned up and went to his side, just like the other bridesmaids with their escorts.

As the soft melody played from the white-rose-decorated reception hall, she tapped him on his shoulder. He turned, his expression impassive, eyes a steely blue.

"You ready?" she asked, smiling until her cheeks hurt. She wasn't going to do anything that ruined this wedding.

"Of course." He offered his arm, and as she tried not to

be affected by how the coldness in his voice stung her, she wrapped her arm around his. A moment passed and he said, "You look beautiful, Maddie."

A pleasant flush swept across her cheeks and down her throat, almost mirroring the crimson Grecian-style dress. Her heart tripped over itself. She glanced at him and their eyes met for a fraction of a second before she tilted her head to the side, letting the stream of hair shield her face.

"Thank you," she whispered. "You look great, too."

He took the compliment in the usual Chase fashion and nodded. Awkward silence stretched out between them and it seemed unbelievable that it had ever been any other way. To be honest, Madison wasn't sure why Chase was giving her the cold shoulder. He was the one who wanted their night to be a one-night stand. He was the one who'd left. All she did was try and salvage a bit of her pride and tell him she agreed. What the heck more did he want from her?

Heart heavy, she lifted her chin as she heard the cue of the music. Before them, each couple entered the hall, smiling. And then it was their turn. From deep inside, she found the happiness and affection she felt for her brother and Lissa. The smile that spread across her face was genuine, even though her heart was breaking inside.

Because after this weekend, she really wouldn't see Chase everywhere like before. A door would be opening this weekend for some while a door would be closing for her.

Each row was full of family and friends. Standing-room only, she realized, overjoyed to know that so many people loved her brother and Lissa. It did wonders for the melancholy that was threatening to rise up and swallow her whole.

The arm around hers tensed halfway down the aisle, and she glanced at Chase. His gaze was questioning and concerned.

But her smile remained throughout the romantic ceremony. Her brother was incredibly cute, turning into this clumsy, near–emotional wreck as he held Lissa's hand and repeated the words that would bind them together, through sickness and health. And when tears filled her eyes, threatening to ruin all the hard work on her mascara and eyeliner, it was because of how truly in love Lissa and her brother were. Her heart swelled and ached at the same time.

The way they kept gazing at each other throughout the ceremony stole her breath and when it came to that moment, when the words *You may now kiss the bride* were spoken, she realized that was what true love looked like.

Clutching the small white rose bouquet in her hands, she sniffed back tears.

Guests shot to their feet and cheered. Tears fell freely, and Madison choked on a small laugh as Mitch swept his arm around the waist of his new wife, dipped her low, and kissed her in a way a sister should never see her brother kissing.

As Lissa and Mitch parted, laughing and smiling at each other, Madison's eyes met Chase's. There was a world of secrets in his gaze, a world that had and always would be locked to her. She'd had the briefest, sweetest taste, and she would savor it.

* * *

Silverware clinked, nearly muted by the laughter and hum of conversation from the main table and the smaller round ones surrounding it.

Chase laughed at something Chad said as he scanned the rows of smiling faces. His eyes stopped on one in particular. Maddie.

Damn, she looked absolutely beautiful. The crimson gown accented her alabaster skin and dark hair, not to mention it clung in all the places that had his blood racing to a certain part of his anatomy. Not that it had stopped racing to that place since he'd first laid eyes on Maddie this weekend.

God, he wanted to take her away, some place private. His fingers burned to skim the heart-shaped neckline. Watch the peaks of her breasts tighten under his gaze, feel the slight tremble as his hand slipped under the gown.

Chase shifted in his seat as he watched her from behind hooded eyes.

A small, tight-lipped smile crossed her delicate features and her eyes seemed to dance under the low lights and candlelight, but he knew something was up with her. He just wished he could figure out where it'd all gone wrong. He could have sworn when he'd gotten up that morning they were both finally on the same page.

Acid gnawed at his belly like no tomorrow. He tried to convince himself that it was an ulcer. Hell, an ulcer would be better than what really had his insides churning and spinning on themselves.

All night, Chase had tossed and turned like he'd drunk a bucket of coffee. Maddie's words lingered with him long after they'd been said. He replayed them over and over again, analyzing them like an obsessive teenage girl. That's what he'd been lowered to. Damn.

Chase leaned back in his seat, idly turning the stem of his flute of champagne.

The way things had been left between them wasn't good, and it made him all kinds of itchy giving her the space she obviously wanted.

He felt like shit, unsure if it were something physical or more. Throughout the day, he'd convinced himself that when he returned to the city, there'd be enough going on to distract him. There was the responsibility of running his clubs to lose himself in; the plans to open a fourth, which meant a lot of meetings to occupy his time; and there were women . . .

Chase's stomach soured at the thought, and he didn't like it.

His gaze slid back to where she sat beside her parents. Shit. He needed to stop staring at her like a lovesick hound. Someone was bound to notice. Hell, people had already noticed, including Mitch.

Against his will and common sense, he was staring at Maddie again, practically willing her to look up and notice him.

And she did.

Chase sucked in a breath, barely aware that Mitch had stood and was giving a toast to his new wife. He wasn't hearing a damn thing except the pulse pounding in his ears. A simple look from her and his body was already coming alive. He was hard as forged steel. Freaking ridiculous. Aw hell, it was more than that—this instantaneous physical reaction that just wouldn't go away.

"To us!" Mitch cheered, holding up his champagne glass. "To our future!"

Madison raised hers, her gaze still locked with his. Her lips moved, mirroring the same words he murmured. "To our future."

Chapter Twelve

Chase woke up Sunday morning, covered in a cold sweat. Either he was coming down with the plague or he was having withdrawals from the pollution and smog of DC.

Or it was something entirely different and it had a name. Maddie.

He rolled onto his side, opening his eyes and squinting at the rays of sun seeping in under the blinds. One look at the clock, and he knew he didn't have a whole lot of time to lie in bed. Mitch and Lissa would be leaving soon for their honeymoon in the Bahamas, and Chase wanted to see them off.

There was also a hidden agenda.

Chase wanted to see Maddie, and he hoped he could corner her before she left for the city. They needed to talk, and with the wedding celebrations over, it would be the perfect time to do so. No distractions. No family or friends lingering around to overhear the conversation. No way for her to escape.

Kicking off the sheets that were twisted around his hips, he stood and stretched. It had taken until the wee hours of the night, but Chase had finally figured out what had Maddie running scared. She'd claimed she just wanted to be friends now, but he was calling bullshit on that. If that were the case, she wouldn't have been so offended when he'd suggested hooking up. And she wouldn't have been his little shadow for the last several years.

No. She was lying. Lying to protect herself, and he got that. After all, he'd done nothing to show her that he felt any differently than what he'd been saying all these years, that he was no better than his father. If anything, he'd proven she was right time and time again. The first time had been the opening of the nightclub.

Stepping under the hot spray of the shower, he cursed. Remembering how delectable she looked in her black dress that night, staring at him with those wide, innocent eyes, and he was hard as a rock.

He had wanted her then, had come so close to taking her right there on the couch in his office. Her brother hadn't been the only thing that had stopped him. Maddie had deserved better than that. But when he pulled back and came to his senses, he couldn't believe what he had almost done. So the next day, like a total ass with good intentions, he'd apologized to her and claimed that he'd been drunk.

Then he'd gone out with every woman who looked nothing like Maddie, just so he could get her out of his head. He'd masked his desire to be near her as something brotherly, when in reality—which he could admit to now—it was a need to be with her.

Placing his hands on the wet tile of the shower, he tipped his head back and closed his eyes. Deep down he'd always known how much he cared for her, that it went beyond affection and into the realm of the big L-word, but he never accepted it, never dared to even acknowledge it.

But now he did, and there was no way he could let her go.

Showered, changed, and determined as hell, he headed up to the main cabin, not surprised to find his brothers and most of the Daniels family there.

Mitch and Lissa were busy saying good-bye while fending off smartass comments from Chase's brothers. His eyes scanned the crowd of waiting people, searching out the face he needed to see most.

But he didn't find her.

Turning to Mr. Daniels, he frowned. "Where's Maddie?"

"You just missed her," he said, looking over his shoulder as Lissa laughed loudly. Mitch had picked her up and was twirling her around. "She said her good-byes and left for the city."

Acid boiled in his stomach. There was no way Maddie would've left without saying good-bye to him. No way. But she had. Maddie had left.

She had left him behind.

Oh, hell no.

Chase hadn't wasted a moment after the happy couple departed for the airport. Hopping in his car, he took off after the little witch. It should've only taken less than an hour to get into the city, but luck had not been on his side.

There was an accident on the toll road that delayed him by forty-five minutes. Then two lanes were closed as he neared the beltway, and another damn accident on the bridge. When he finally parked his car in the garage behind the Gallery, he'd killed the engine and all but ran to the entrance. She could run from him, she could hide all she wanted, but she would see the truth. They couldn't be friends.

It wasn't enough. It could never be enough.

Maddie had one of the smaller apartments on the lower floors, and he was too impatient to wait for the elevator to come down, so he took the stairs, bum-rushing them like a lunatic.

He didn't care.

All he could think was that Maddie had left without saying good-bye. His Maddie would've never done that. She would have stayed and screamed at him. Railed at him. Hell, even slapped him in the face. But no way would she have run unless she was scared and not angry.

Heart pumping, he pushed open the door to the fourth floor, nearly plowing into a young couple with their ankle-biter dog.

"Sorry," he muttered, hurrying past them. Reaching Maddie's door, he stopped and banged on it like he was the police about to rain down hell on someone. "Maddie? It's Chase."

No answer.

Growing irritated with the minx, he rapped his knuckles on the door, seriously considering kicking it in. He doubted she'd appreciate that.

Across the hall, a door opened to an apartment Chase knew had been up for lease. The superintendent stepped out, covered in paint-splattered overalls.

"Is everything okay, Mr. Gamble?" he asked, using a cloth to wipe his hands.

Only then did he realize he really did look like a madman beating on Maddie's door. He lowered his hand and cleared his throat. "I was looking for Maddie."

The superintendent smiled fondly. "Miss Daniels isn't home. She's out with the realtor, checking into some town-homes across the river."

Chase's heart tipped over heavily. "A realtor?"

He nodded. "Yeah, Miss Daniels called me yesterday, letting me know she was planning on moving. Something about getting out of the city. I hate to hear that she's leaving, since she's such a great tenant, but I hooked her up with a realtor we use. Seemed like she wanted to do this fast."

None of it made sense. His brain outright refused to believe it. She adored the city and loved the fact that there was next to no commute to work. She would never leave this city. It wasn't her—unless . . .

As he stared at the superintendent, disbelief gave way to a pain so real he was surprised he hadn't dropped to his knees. The knowledge sunk in slowly, twisting his guts and turning him inside out. She wasn't just gone. It was more than simply hiding from him.

She was determined to leave him before he had a chance to really ever have her.

Madison sat at her desk Monday morning, frowning as she scanned through the hundred e-mails she'd missed while at the vineyard. Nothing too important, but she clicked on the first one and started to methodically read through it.

Having no idea how much time had passed, she glanced up when Bridget placed a steaming latte on her desk. She smiled. "Thank you. I so need this."

"I can tell." Bridget sat on the edge of Madison's desk, holding her drink in one hand and fiddling with her pens with the other. No doubt she'd separate them by color. Blue in one holder. Black in the other. "You look like you haven't slept in a week."

Self-consciously smoothing a hand over her low ponytail, she winced. She'd already filled Bridget in on what had happened at the wedding and her plans for the future.

"I met with a realtor yesterday afternoon and we checked out some townhomes in Virginia." She paused, hating how hard it was to even say those words. "I was out pretty late." And she also hadn't slept well last night. She loved her apartment—she loved the city—but this had to be done. There was no way she could stay this close to Chase anymore, risk running into him out with one of his turnstile girlfriends. It would kill her.

Bridget shook her head. "I can't believe you're moving."

She shrugged as she ran her finger over the thin scratch in the desk's surface. "I think it's time for a change in scenery."

Her friend looked doubtful. "And it has nothing to do with who shares the same apartment building as you? Or the whole tempting the best man?"

Madison flushed but said nothing.

"I know it's hard for you to see him, but Madison . . . moving away?" Bridget sighed. "I'm not sure that's the right move to make."

She had her doubts, too, but she'd made up her mind. "I need a fresh start, Bridget. And the only way I'm going to get that is by getting away from him as much as I possibly can. If I have to keep seeing him, I'm never going to get over him."

A sympathetic look crossed Bridget's features. "What are you going to do about family functions?"

"Other than hope he doesn't show up?" She took a sip of her latte. "Deal with it? I don't think it will be so bad when I'm not seeing him every freaking day."

"Hmm. You know, for some people, distance makes the heart fonder."

"Yeah, well, those people need to be hog-tied and shot." Madison set her drink down on her desk and toyed with her mouse. "It's a drastic move, I know, but I need to do this."

And she did. Like she'd just told Bridget, she'd never fully get over Chase if she had to keep seeing him; hearing about his exploits; and, at times, witnessing them. Moving out of the city would help.

All in all she didn't regret what had happened during the wedding. That night was something she'd cherish for a long time, probably for as long as she lived. And maybe one day, she'd find that kind of passion again. Her chest ached at the thought and a hard lump formed in the back of her throat, but she couldn't force someone to love her.

"Well, at least the wedding was beautiful, right?" Bridget said, returning to the desk she shared in Madison's office.

Madison nodded. "It was a wedding to remember, for sure."

"Sounds like a Hallmark card." Bridget laughed as

Madison went back to thumbing through her e-mails. "You should write that one down. It would make for a corny—oh, holy crap."

Looking up, Madison frowned at her friend. "What?"

Bridget's blue eyes were wide. "Uh, take a look for yourself."

Confused, Madison followed Bridget's gaze and her mouth dropped open. "Oh my God . . ."

Through the glass walls surrounding her office, there was no mistaking the dark head prowling directly toward her or the broad shoulders squared with intent and determination.

Chase.

What was he doing here? Why? There wasn't any time for her to come up with those answers, because her door flew open and Chase stood there, tall, dark, sinfully sexy, and a whole lot pissed off.

Madison started to stand, but her legs were too weak. "Chase, what are you doing here?"

Fire lit his eyes as they landed on her. "We need to talk."

"Uh, right now?" She looked around her office helplessly. "I think it—"

"It can't wait," he all but growled. "We need to talk now."

Bridget started to stand. "I think I'll give you guys some privacy. There are other desks out there I'm sure need organizing."

Madison was already on her feet, smoothing her hands down the cotton of her skirt. Over Chase's shoulder, she could see plenty of her co-workers staring from their cubicles. This was going to get awkward. "No. You don't have to leave. Um, Chase and I can—"

Before she could finish her sentence, he was in front of her. Without saying a word, he clasped her cheeks and brought his mouth to hers. Too stunned to react at first, she froze as his lips pressed, slowly demanding that her mouth open to his. Then her body melted into his embrace, into the kiss that quickly deepened.

He pulled her against him, lifting her onto the toes of her shoes. He kissed her with all the passion and desperate yearning she had carried with her for so many years. The way his arms trembled against hers reached deep inside, shattering the freshly built walls around her heart.

When he pulled back, he kept his arms around her. "Why . . . why did you do that?" she asked.

A small half grin played across his face. "Sorry. I had to get that out of the way first."

"Wow. I need popcorn for this," Bridget murmured.

Madison flushed from the roots of her hair to the tips of her curled toes. Somehow, she had forgotten that her friend was still standing there . . . plus an entire room full of people watching from the outside through the glass walls. Pulling back, she shook her head. "Chase . . ."

"Let me explain something first, okay? Before you run off or start arguing with me."

"I—"

"Maddie," he said, eyes glittering.

"You better let the man talk." Bridget sat back down in her chair, folding her arms. "I cannot wait to hear what he has to say."

Madison shot her friend a death glare, but it looked like she wasn't going anywhere. Neither was he. "Okay," she said.

Chase took a long breath. "There's no way around saying this, other than just coming straight out with it. I've been an idiot—an ass. Time and time again, I've done the wrong thing by you."

Her mouth dropped open.

"And this whole time I'd been trying to do the right thing by not being with you. I didn't want to betray Mitch by hooking up with his little sister. I didn't want to somehow mess up our friendship, either, because you have been such a huge part of my life." He took a deep breath. "And I never wanted to be like my father—to treat you like he treated my mom. And it was stupid—I get that now. Chad was right. Father never loved our mother, but it's different for me—it's different for us. It always has been."

The whole time he spoke, he never looked away from her. She opened her mouth to say something but he rushed ahead. "But all I've managed to do is screw things up. That night in the club . . . I wasn't drunk."

Madison shifted uncomfortably. "I know."

"It was a lame excuse, and I'm sorry. That night—I should've told you how I really felt. And every night thereafter," he said, taking a step forward. "I should've told you how I felt the night in that damn cabin, too."

Her heart swelled as hope grew in a tangle of emotions she could never unravel. All of this seemed surreal. Tears rushed her eyes as she reached behind her, grasping the edges of her desk. "And how do you feel?"

Chase's smile revealed those deep dimples she loved, and when he spoke, his voice was husky. "Aw hell, Maddie, I'm not good at this kind of stuff. You . . . you are my world. You've always been my world, ever since I can remember."

At Bridget's soft inhale, Madison placed a trembling hand over her mouth.

Stepping forward, he placed a hand over hers, gently pulling it away from her mouth. "It's the truth. You are my everything. I love you. I have for longer than I realized. Please tell me my boneheadedness hasn't screwed things up beyond repair for us."

Madison didn't move for a moment, didn't even breathe as his words tumbled inside her and wrapped their way around her heart, just as his strong fingers were wrapping around hers. And then she sprang forward, planting her lips right on his.

He kissed her back desperately and passionately, his arms crushing her to his chest. She could feel the hard heat of him, from the tips of her breasts down to the harder, hotter part of him pressed against her belly. She reveled in his arousal, in the passion in which he held her—even though this so was not the place for it—but she did, because this was the moment she'd been waiting for her whole life.

This was it. The lump was back in her throat. She barely realized Bridget had quietly slipped out of the office.

"I want you," he rasped against her lips.

Her breath caught. "You do?"

Chase nodded. "There is no one else—there's never been anyone else for me but you. You're it, Maddie. And I swear to you, I will never treat you like my father did my mom. Hell, I couldn't. I'm just not built like that man."

Blinking back hot tears, she wrapped her arms around

Chase and breathed in the scent of him. "Oh, God, Chase, I love you so much."

His laugh was a mixture of relief and joy as he held her tighter, and she could feel his heart thundering against hers. She placed her lips near his ear and whispered, "I think I need to use a sick day, because there's something I really want to do right now."

Chase's breath left in an unsteady rush. "I couldn't agree more, but . . ."

"But?" Madison pulled back with a frown.

He grinned at her. "But afterward we're going to your parents' house."

"We are?" A smile swept across her lips. Giddy, she looped her arms around his neck. "I'm afraid to even ask."

Chase's smile matched hers. "I think we need to break the news to your parents face-to-face, because this . . ." He kissed her again, his tongue tangling with hers, drawing a breathy moan. And that kiss went on until her toes curled inside her heels and her heart thudded heavily in her chest.

Kissing Chase—loving Chase—was something she'd never get tired of.

Pulling back, his mouth formed a smile against hers and he said, "This is forever."

Acknowledgments

Acknowledgements are always difficult to write. No matter how many people I thank, I know I'm always forgetting someone. So this time, I'll keep it short and sweet, just like Chase would. Thank you to everyone who has had a supportive or kind thing to say, to those behind the scenes who helped *Tempting the Best Man* become a reality, and to those who will share Maddie and Chase's journey.

Enjoyed reading *Tempting the Best Man?*
Here's an extract from the scorchingly sexy
second novel in the Gamble Brothers series,
Tempting the Player.

Chapter One

As Bridget Rodgers stared at the old meat-packing warehouse, she kept seeing flashes of the movie *Hostel* in her head. According to her friend, the invite-only, highly gossiped about Leather and Lace club was the place to be. But from the cemented-over windows and graffiti-sprayed exterior walls, in what were probably gang symbols, plus the dim flickering light from the nearby lamppost, Bridget figured most patrons of this club ended up on missing persons posters or on the evening news.

"I can't believe I let you talk me into this, Shell. We're probably going to become some perverted rich man's victim by midnight." Bridget straightened the thick leather belt around the waist of her dress. The belt was purple, of course, and her sweater dress a deep red. Her signature look was a bit gaudy, but at least it would help the police identify her body later.

Shell passed her a droll look. "You don't even want to know what I had to do to get an invite to this club." She waved the business card–sized paper in front of Bridget's face. "We're going to have fun doing something different. Boo on the local watering holes."

For all the hoopla surrounding Leather and Lace, one would think it would be in a better location than Foggy Bottom. With the creepy, unsightly look to it and the fog rolling in every night, it seemed doubtful the place catered to the rich and powerful in DC.

The club had become sort of an urban legend, and the name probably had something to do with it. Leather and Lace. Seriously? Who thought that was a good idea? Supposedly, it was a sex club. A means of hooking up people with "mutual interests," like Match.com for the sexually wild or something, but Bridget didn't really believe it. And if it was, oh well. In reality, all clubs and bars catered to sex in one way or another. It was why half the single people went out on the weekend.

It was why she used to go out on the weekend.

"Come on, get the sourpuss look off your face," Shell said. "You need something fun and new. You *need* to de-stress."

"Getting drunk—"

"And hopefully getting laid," Shell added with a wicked grin.

Bridget's laugh sent puffs of small white clouds into the air. "That's so not going to fix my problems."

"True, but they will definitely take your mind off them."

She did need some good old-fashioned stress relief, though. As much as she loved her job and really wanted to go cry in the corner at the thought of finding something else, it wasn't covering her bills—namely the student loans—that were taking a huge chunk out of her monthly income. She'd come to loathe when her phone rang, and it was an eight hundred number.

Sallie Mae was a freaking vulture.

She sighed as she glanced back at the building. That *was* a gang sign. "So how did you score an invite to this place?"

"It's really not that exciting," Shell said, frowning at the card she held.

"All right," Bridget said, squaring her shoulders as she turned to her friend. The shorter girl was shivering in her skintight black mini and Bridget smiled. Sometimes having extra padding had its benefits. Early October air was chilly, but her knees weren't knocking. "If this place is lame or if anyone tries to pry out my eyeball, we're leaving pronto."

Shell nodded solemnly. "Deal."

Their heels echoed off the cracked pavement as they hurried toward what appeared to be the front entrance. Once they got within seeing distance of the tiny square window in the door, it swung open, revealing a pro wres-tler–sized man in a black T-shirt.

"Card," he barked.

Shell stepped forward, holding the card out. The bouncer took it, scanned it over quickly, and then asked for IDs, which he scanned and handed back. When he held the door wider, it appeared they'd passed the popularity and age test.

Then again, both of them were pushing twenty-seven and could no longer be confused with underage drinkers anymore. Sigh. Growing old sucked sometimes.

The entrance to the club was a narrow hallway with track lighting. The walls were black. The ceiling was black. The door up ahead was black. Bridget's soul was dying a little at the lack of color and splash.

When they arrived at the second door, it too opened,

showing another big dude in . . . a black T-shirt. Bridget was starting to detect a theme here. Shell gave a little squeal as she slid past the second bouncer, giving him a long look, which was returned threefold.

Bridget's first glance around the main floor of the club was impressive. Whoever had designed this place had done well. Nothing inside gave an indication that this used to be a warehouse.

Lighting was dim, but not the shady kind of lighting that everyone looked good in at three a.m. A girl sometimes just couldn't catch a break. Several large tables surrounded a raised dance floor that would be treacherous as hell getting up and down from while drunk, but it was packed with bodies. Large, long couches lined walls painted in blood red. A spiral staircase led to the second floor but there, bouncers were blocking the top landing.

From what Bridget could see, there looked to be private alcoves up there. She bet there were a whole lot of shenanigans going on in those shadowy cubbyholes.

Behind the staircase was a sprawling bar run by eight bartenders. Never in her life had she seen so many bartenders actually working at once. Four men. Four women. All of them dressed in black, mixing drinks and chatting with the patrons.

The place was busy but not overly packed like most of the clubs in the city. And instead of stale cigarette smoke, beer, and body odor, there was a clove-like scent in the air.

This place was definitely not bad.

Shell spun toward her, clutching her black clutch in her

hand. "Tonight is going to be a night you never forget. Mark my words."

Bridget smiled.

Another shot made its way from Chad Gamble's hand to his mouth. The bite of alcohol watered his eyes, but like any family with a real good alcoholic circling around, it would take an entire keg of this shit to get him drunk.

And by the looks of those at the club tonight, getting drunk instead of laid was looking more and more like the outcome. Not one female had caught his attention. Sure, plenty of beautiful women had approached him and his friend Tony.

But Chad wasn't interested.

And Tony was more caught up in giving Chad shit than anything else. "Man, you've got to calm this crap down. You keep ending up in the papers, the Club's gonna come down on you like a ton of bricks."

Chad groaned as he leaned forward, motioning at Bartender Jim. He wasn't sure if that was his real name or not, but hell, he'd been calling the man that for about two years now and never been corrected.

"Another?" Bartender Jim asked.

Chad glanced at Tony and sighed. "Make it two shots."

The bartender chuckled as he reached down, grabbing a bottle of Grey Goose. "I have to side with Tony on this. Signing a contract with the Yankees makes you a traitor to half the world."

Chad rolled his eyes. "Or it makes me smart and incredibly career oriented?"

"It makes your agent a greedy bastard," Tony replied, thrumming his fingers off the top of the bar. "You and I both know the Nationals are paying you enough."

Bartender Jim snorted.

The Nationals were paying him more than enough— enough that by the time retirement age came around, he'd be more than set. Hell, he had more money now than he even knew what to do with, but at thirty, he had another six years left in his pitching arm, maybe more. Right now he was still in his prime. He had it all—God-given skill with a wicked fastball and precise aim; experience with the game; and, as his agent put it, a face that actually drew women to baseball games.

But the money and the contract offers rolling in weren't the problem with the Nationals.

Chad was—or his "hard partying lifestyle" or whatever the gossip column had called it. According to the *Post*, Chad had a different woman every night and while that sounded damn fun, it was far from the truth. Unfortunately, he had enough relationships that whatever was written about him was believed by the masses. His reputation was as well known as his pitching arm.

But when fans were more concerned with whom he was screwing instead of how the team was playing, it was bad news.

The Nationals wanted to keep him on, which was what Chad wanted, too. He loved this town—the team and coaches. His life was here—his brothers and the Daniels family, who had been like parents to him. Leaving the city meant saying good-bye to them, but the team demanded that he "settle down."

Settle the fuck down, like he was some kind of wild college kid. Settle down? Sure, he'd settle what he'd been told was a rather fine ass in this barstool.

Chad took the shot, slamming the glass back down. "I'm not going anywhere, Tony. You know that."

"Good to hear." Tony paused. "But what if the Nationals don't re-sign you?"

"They'll re-sign me."

Tony shook his head. "You better hope they don't get wind of what went down in that hotel room on Wednesday night."

Chad laughed. "Man, you were with me Wednesday night and you know damn well nothing went down in that hotel room."

His friend snickered. "And who's going to believe that if those three ladies say differently? And yeah, I know calling them 'ladies' is stretching it, but with your reputation, the Club will believe anything. You just need to keep a low profile."

"A low profile?" Chad snorted. "Maybe you didn't understand me. They don't want me to keep a low profile. They want me to *settle down*."

"Hell," Tony muttered. "Well, it's not like they're asking you to get married."

Chad shot him a look. "Actually, I'm pretty sure they want me to find 'a nice girl' and 'stay out of clubs' and—"

"Clubs like this one?" Tony chuckled.

"Exactly," he said. "I need to revamp my whole image, whatever the hell my image is."

Tony shrugged. "You're a player, Chad. Stop being a player."

Chad opened his mouth. Well, he really couldn't argue against that statement. Settling down was not in the Gamble brothers' vocab. His brother Chase didn't count anymore. Traitor. Chad loved his soon-to-be sister-in-law Maddie and she was great for Chase, but Chad and their other brother, Chandler, were not going to find themselves shackled to any female anytime soon.

"If you say 'don't hate the player, hate the game,' I'm going to knock you out of your seat," Tony warned.

He laughed. "You need to screw or something. Get some of that angst out of your ass. Even if I decide to go with another team, I'm not breaking up with you."

Tony flipped him off as his dark eyes scanned the floor behind them. His friend leaned back suddenly, lips pursing. "Ah, I've never seen these two before. Interesting . . ."

Chad twisted at the waist, searching down to find what had caught Tony's interest. Must be something pretty damn good because his friend was as bored with the night's offerings as he was.

His eyes scanned over a tall, slender blonde with a leather choker, dancing with a shorter woman. They were staring directly at Chad and Tony, but they were regulars. He checked out a few more women but wasn't seeing anything new. He started to turn back around when he caught sight of hair the color of dark wine.

Damn. He always had a thing for redheads.

Chad turned around fully.

The woman was standing next to a blonde who was placing a drink on one of the high tables, but his eyes went back to the redhead. She was tall—her head would probably come up to his shoulders, and he was a good six and a half feet standing straight. Her skin was like unblemished porcelain, fair and easily flushed. He couldn't tell what color her eyes were from here, but he was betting they were green or hazel. Her lips were pouty, shaped like a bow; the kind of mouth that begged to be claimed and then would haunt men's dreams long afterward.

Chad's gaze dipped and, oh hells yes, his dick, which hadn't been active all night, stirred to life. The red dress ended just below the elbows and above the knees, but he saw enough to know he liked—a lot. The material stretched across her full breasts. Chad wanted to take off the belt around her waist and use it for other things. She was rocking the kind of body pin-up models of the fifties showed off—a true woman's body. One that demanded hands and tongues trace the curves of, if they dared, and, oh yeah, he dared.

"Hot damn," Chad murmured.

Tony chuckled deeply. "The redhead, huh? Saw her first. Bet she could handle just about anything thrown her way."

Chad cut his friend a dark look. "The redhead is mine."

"Oh, simmer down, boy." Tony raised his hands in mock surrender. "I like the blonde, too."

He held Tony's gaze long enough for his friend to get that he wasn't fucking around before he turned his attention back to the redhead. She was sitting at the table now, fiddling with the straw in her drink. One of the regulars stopped by her table—Joe something or another—making a beeline for the fresh meat. Joe worked for the government, doing fuck knows what. Chad never had a problem with the guy before, but it took everything in his self-control not to get up and physically remove him.

Joe said something and the blonde laughed. The redhead flushed, and now Chad was hard as freaking granite. Man, he wanted to know if that flush traveled down and how far it went. No—he *needed* to know. His life depended on it.

"Fuck," he said, glancing at Tony. "Have I told you how much I think Joe is an asshole?"

Tony chuckled. "No, but I can guess why you think so."

Nodding absently, his eyes narrowed on the redhead. Whoever she was, she wasn't going home with Joe tonight. She was going home with *him*.

Chapter Two

The people who frequented Leather and Lace were . . . *friendly*. Already, two different men and a woman had stopped by their table, chatting casually and openly flirting. If Bridget were into girls, the flaxen-haired beauty who'd been eyeing Shell would've definitely done it for her, but the two men barely sparked any interest, which was weird, because they were good-looking and charming. One of them had showered her with a lot of attention, but she was feeling oh so very meh about it.

There was a good chance her vagina was broken or something.

Sighing, she finished off her drink while Shell practiced her seduction technique on some dark-haired guy named Bill or Will. The heady thrum of music easing out of the speakers made it difficult to hear what they were saying to each other, but the odds Bridget would be calling a cab later tonight were high.

Or worse, even using the Metro, which she was convinced was one of Dante's circles of hell.

When she got home, she'd dive into that Reese's pie she discovered in the local market earlier and that book she'd totally stolen off of Maddie's desk when she'd left work. Bridget had no idea what it was about, but the cover was green—she loved the color green—and the dude on the cover was hot. Oh, and she needed to feed Pepsi, the alley cat she'd found in a Pepsi box when he was a kitten.

Wait.

It was a Friday night, she was at a club, and a good-looking man was currently giving her the I-want-to-take-you-home-and-I-hope-I-last-longer-than-five-minutes look . . . and she was thinking about pie, a young adult book, and feeding her cat.

She was so turning into the cat lady at twenty-seven. Sweet.

"I'm heading to the bar," Bridget announced, thinking she could at least be drunk and not care how her evening turned out. "Either of you two want a refill?"

Bridget waited for a response, but after a few seconds, she rolled her eyes and stood. Picking up her mauve clutch, she slipped around the table and headed toward the bar. It had gotten fuller since they'd arrived. Squeezing in next to a woman with short, spiky black hair, she leaned against the bar.

Surprisingly, a bartender seemed to appear out of thin air. "What can I get you, sweetie?"

Sweetie? How . . . sweet. "Rum and Coke."

"Coming right up."

Bridget smiled her thanks as she glanced down the bar. Several people were paired off, a few were alone or chatting with those standing by the bar. She caught sight of a guy with dark hair and eyes and thought she'd seen him before.

A tall glass was placed in front of her and she opened her clutch, reaching for some cash.

"I have it covered," a deep and smooth voice intruded. A large hand landed on the bar beside her. "Put it on my tab."

The bartender turned to help someone else before Bridget could politely refuse. Accepting drinks from strangers was a no-go for her. Candy was a different story.

She turned halfway, her gaze following those long fingers to where a dark sweater's sleeve was rolled up to the elbow. The material clung to a thick, well-muscled upper arm, which connected to broad shoulders she found vaguely familiar. Whoever the guy was, he was exceptionally tall. Nearing six feet herself, she had to tip her head back to meet his eyes, and that made her all kinds of giddy.

Though the moment she saw his face, all giddiness vanished, replaced by about a thousand different emotions she couldn't even begin to separate. She *knew* him. Not just because everyone in the city knew who he was, but she *really* knew him.

One didn't forget a face like his or the qualities he shared with his brothers. Wide, expressive lips that looked firm and unyielding. Dominant. The curve of his jaw was strong and his cheekbones broad. His nose was slightly crooked from taking a ball in the face three years ago. Somehow the imperfection only made him sexier. Thick, coal black lashes framed eyes the color of the deepest ocean water. His dark brown hair was cropped short on the sides and longer on the top, styled in a messy spike that made him look like he'd just rolled out of bed.

Chad mother-freaking Gamble. All-star pitcher for the Nationals, middle Gamble brother, and older brother to one Chase Gamble, who just happened to be the boyfriend of her boss/coworker Madison Daniels.

Holy crapola.

She'd heard a lot about him from Madison. Part of her felt like she even knew him. Her friend had grown up with the Gamble brothers and been in love with one of them her whole life, but Bridget had never seen Chad out and about, at least not up close like this. They didn't run in the same circles, obviously. And he was here, at a club rumored to be all about sex, and he'd bought *her* a drink?

Was he confused? Drunk? Took too many balls to the face? And dear sweet Mary mother of baby Jesus, that was a fine-looking face.

Based on what Maddie had said about him and what the gossips reported in the papers, Chase was a well-known womanizer. Bridget had seen in the rags the women he was out and about with. All tall and insanely gorgeous models, and definitely not women who were entertaining thoughts of pie and paranormal books.

But he was looking at her like he knew what he was doing. Color her surprised and intrigued. "Thank you," she finally managed after staring at him for God knew how long like a total goober.

Chad's easy grin created a flutter deep in her belly. "My pleasure. I haven't noticed you before. My name is—"

"I know who you are." Bridget flushed hotly. Now she sounded like an über stalker. She considered telling him how she knew, but on a whim decided to just see where this went. There was a good chance once he knew of their six degrees of separation—aka "I might run into you again someday"—relationship, he might just offer her a wave goodbye. This player was not known for his longevity anywhere except on the field. "I mean, I know *of* you. Chad Gamble."

The grin went up a notch. "Well, you have me at a disadvantage. I don't know you."

Still flushing, she turned and picked up her drink, needing a healthy dose of liquid courage. "Bridget Rodgers."

"Bridget," he repeated, and good Lord in heaven, the way he said her name was like he *tasted* it. "I like the name."

She had no idea what to say, which was shocking. Normally the social butterfly, she was thrown for a loop. Why was he, surely a god among men, talking to her? Taking a sip, she cursed her sudden inept ability at conversation.

Chad eased in between her and an unoccupied stool behind him. Their bodies were so close that she caught the scent of spice and soap. "Is rum and Coke your favorite drink?" he asked.

Letting out a nervous breath, she nodded. "I'm a fan of it, but vodka is also a go-to drink."

"Ah, a woman after my own heart." His gaze dipped to her lips and her body warmed as tension formed deep inside her. "Well, when you finish with your rum and Coke, we'll have to share a shot of vodka."

She tucked her hair behind her ear, fighting what was probably a big, goofy smile. Though she doubted this conversation was going anywhere, she was big enough to admit she liked the attention. "That sounds like a plan."

"Good." His gaze moved back up to her eyes, meeting hers and holding for a moment. He leaned in, lowering his head. "Guess what?" he said in a conspiratorial whisper.

"What?"

"The seat behind you just opened." He winked, and damn if he didn't look good doing it. "And there's one open behind me. I think it's telling us something."

Laughing softly, she couldn't fight the smile then. "And what is that?"

"You and I should sit and chat."

Her heart was thumping in her chest in a crazy and fun sort of way, reminding her of what it had been like when she was younger and the boy she'd been crushing on talked to her at a party. But this was different. Chad was different. There was a wealth of heat in his eyes when he looked at her.

Bridget glanced over to the table where Shell was still with the guy Bridget couldn't remember was called Bill or Will. "Well then, we must listen to the cosmos."

She sat and Chad followed suit, scooting the barstool over under the guise of being able to hear her better, but she knew differently. This wasn't her first time at the rodeo when it came to meeting men at bars, but Chad was ridiculously smooth. None of what he'd said sounded cheesy. His voice dripped with cool confidence and something else she couldn't put her finger on.

Sitting so close, his knee pressed into her thigh. "So, what do you do, Bridget?"

She started to say where she worked but decided against it. The fact that she knew Maddie and Chase would definitely change things. "I work downtown as an executive assistant. I know. I know. That's a glorified term for a secretary, but I love what I do."

Chad placed an arm on the counter, toying with the neck of his beer bottle. "Hey, as long as it's something you enjoy, doesn't matter what it is."

"Do you still enjoy playing baseball?" At the weird look that crossed his face, she added, "I mean, you always hear professional players either love or hate the game after a while."

"Ah, I get what you mean. I still love the game. Politics of it, not so much, but I wouldn't change what I do. I get to play and get paid for it."

"Politics?" she asked, curious.

"The behind-the-scenes stuff," he explained, taking a swig of his beer. "Agents. Managers. Contracts. All that stuff doesn't really interest me."

Bridget nodded, wondering what he thought about the heated debate going on in the sports column lately about whether or not he'd take the New York contract. She really didn't follow baseball, only ended up reading the section during a particularly boring lunch one day. Typically, she made a beeline for the gossip page, which always had a hefty amount of info on Chad, now that she thought about it.

As she finished her drink, he peppered her with questions about her background, seeming genuinely interested in what she said. When she asked him about his schooling, she pretended she didn't know what high school and college he went to, but she knew. They were the same as Madison's.

"So, you come here often?" she asked when there was a lull in conversation. Her gaze dipped to his mouth. She was having a hard time not looking there and imagining what his lips would feel like against hers, how he tasted.

"Once a month, sometimes more or less." he explained. "My friend Tony probably comes more."

Now she knew why the dark-haired guy looked familiar. Another baseball player. "Does the entire team come here a lot?"

Chad laughed deeply. "No, most of the guys aren't into this kind of thing."

"Oh? But you are?" Yeah, she assumed some of the guys were probably married.

"Most definitely." He leaned over, placing his arm on the back of her stool. "So you're not originally from the DC area?"

"Nope, I hail from Pennsylvania."

"Pennsylvania lost a treasure."

"Ha. Ha," she said, but she was secretly flattered. Of course, she'd take that fact to the grave. "And you were doing so well before that line."

Chad chuckled. "In this case, I meant what I said, but I agree. That line was bad." His face took on the shape of someone exaggerating being deep in thought, his finger tapping his chin. "Hmm. What's a better line? How about . . ."

"No, no," she said. "Let's forget about better lines. What's your worst line? That sounds like way more fun."

"My *worst* line?" His eyes twinkled. "You're assuming I *have* a worst line, aren't you?"

Bridget gestured at the bar around her with one hand while leaning closer, settling her chin on her other hand, her arm resting on the bar in what she hoped was a seductive pose. She was a little out of practice. "Given you've admitted you hang out here a lot, why yes, I do believe you have many worse lines in you, playa playa." And then she winked. She actually winked. She sincerely hoped he wasn't going to call her out for her worst flirting moves ever because she was pretty sure she'd just emptied the vault in one shebang.

Chad laughed deep and throaty, the sound thrumming down her spine. "Well, I wouldn't want to waste my worst lines on someone as sexy as you."

Bridget couldn't help it—she snorted with laughter. "Well played, sir. Well. Played." And now she was grinning like an idiot, but at least his grin made a matching set. Man, she'd forgotten how fun it was to just get out and flirt with a smart, sexy guy.

He gave a mock bow. "I try."

Two shots of vodka arrived mysteriously. Chad laughed when she had to do the shot in two gulps.

"Cheater," he teased, eyes dancing.

Waving a hand in her face, she laughed. "I don't know how you do it. That stuff is strong."

"Years of practice."

"It's good to see that you excel at something other than baseball."

His gaze settled on her lips. "I excel at many things."

Chad motioned to the bartender for a glass of water and then slid it to her. She gave him a grateful smile and took a sip.

Like one of the women in the romance books she read, she was snared in his gaze. "You know, one more line and you win a set of steak knives."

He leaned in and it felt like there was no room. Her heart sped up as his smile turned half secretive, half playful. "Many, *many* things."

Bridget flushed, blaming the alcohol. "I think you should know, I'm impervious to bar bullshit." She wasn't, of course, as her racing heart clearly proved, but damn if she didn't care.

He reached out, brushing his knuckles along her warm cheek. She shivered. "I like the way you blush."

Bridget felt even more crimson sweep across her cheeks as she reached for her water. "Hey, I thought we agreed no more bad pickup lines." Peeking at him, she found him watching her intently. Actually, she was pretty sure he hadn't taken his eyes off her longer than a few seconds.

"Well, that's no fun." But his eyes were still crinkled with laughter. His gaze flicked to the bartender. "Another drink?"

When she nodded, she ordered something with less punch to it. They resumed talking and before Bridget knew it, she had completely lost sight of Shell as the crowd in the club thickened around the bar, obscuring the view of the tables. Chad had moved closer, his entire leg now pressed against hers. The contact made her skin tingle beneath her dress.

Glancing away, her gaze found a couple dancing nearby—if you called what they were doing dancing. It was basically sex standing up with clothes on. The woman's short denim skirt was pushed high and her leg curled along the narrow slant of the man's hips. Her partner's hand was under the frayed hem as their hips grinded together. She swallowed and turned back to her drink.

"I can't believe I'm giving you my A-game here and you're calling foul ball. I'm wounded," he said, placing a hand over his heart in mock pain.

The teasing tone brought a grin to her lips. "I can tell you have self-esteem issues."

Chad laughed, the sound deep and rumbling before slowly waning off. He leaned in, his expression growing serious for the first time that night. "Can I be honest with you, Bridget?"

She arched a brow. "Do I want you to be?"

His palm traced her wildly beating pulse, his long fingers wrapping around the nape of her neck. "I saw you before you saw me. I came to this side of the bar just to talk to you."

All coherent thought fled her. Was Chad serious? And how much had he been drinking before they met up? It wasn't that she had a low self-esteem. Bridget knew she was pretty, but she also knew her body went out of fashion several decades ago and this club was packed with super-model type chicks. The kind she saw him pictured with time and time again.

But it *was* her he was talking to, touching.

Their lips were so close that their breath mingled. The steady hum of raucous conversation and music around them faded. Maybe it was the alcohol or the fact that it was Chad Gamble. Like any woman with ovaries, she had her fair share of fantasies surrounding the playboy, but everything felt surreal. She was hyperaware of what was happening and at the same time detached from logic.

"And just to be clear, that was not a line." Chad's head tilted to the side. "I want to kiss you."

Chapter Three

"Now?" Bridget's muscles tensed and then immediately relaxed under his skilled ministrations.

"Now."

Bridget's head was tipping back, her body relaxing into his touch, pressing toward it, yielding to it. Chad was spinning a seductive web around her, blurring reality. Her throat was dry and his fingers . . . his fingers were guiding her head back farther and an ache had started in the pit of her stomach. "I . . ."

"Just a kiss." His breath danced over her cheek, and her eyes drifted shut. Bridget's hands opened and closed uselessly in her lap.

Kissing Chad in a packed bar shouldn't turn her on as much as it did. PDA wasn't something she regularly indulged in and usually made fun of when she saw it in public, especially when it was Madison and Chase because they were all over each other constantly, but this . . . this was different and before she knew what she was doing, she said yes.

Bridget didn't feel his lips on hers like she expected.

The tip of his nose brushed over the curve of her jaw,

causing her breath to catch, and then his head dipped lower. With Bridget's head tipped back, her throat was exposed to him. Her hands clenched and then his hot mouth was against where her pulse pounded.

Bridget's entire body jerked as if he were doing something far more wicked than what was usually considered a sweet gesture. The kiss was quick, but as he started to lift his head, he nipped at her neck and then she felt his tongue sweep across her skin, soothing the sting. A moan escaped her parted lips.

"See? It was just a kiss," he said, his voice deep and husky.

Her lashes fluttered open, and Chad was staring down at her, his eyes hooded. "That . . ."

His smug smile spread as he brushed his lips over hers, feather light, making her gasp. "That was? Good?"

"Very nice," she murmured.

He chuckled, and his lips brushed hers once more. "Well, I have to do better than *nice*."

Her heart doubled its beat.

His hair brushed along the underside of her chin, soft as silk, and her fingers itched to touch them, but she didn't dare move. Chad's fingers had slipped through the mass of hair, and his hand was now cradling the back of her head.

There was a moment, so full of anticipation and the unknown, that Bridget's heart stuttered, and then his mouth was against her pulse again and her body tensed tight. His lips were warm and smooth, and she got lost in the feel of them. His tongue circled the area he'd kissed, and then he moved on, trailing tiny kisses down her neck. He nipped at the skin gently, and she jerked. He repeated the tiny scrape of teeth as he went to the hollow between her neck and shoulder, chuckling against her skin when she gasped again.

"Was that very nice?" he asked.

Breathing rapidly, she squeezed her hands into fists. "It was good."

His mouth moved against that tender spot. "You're killing me, Bridget. We have to do better than good or nice."

Chad's mouth was pushing aside the wide scoop collar, exposing more skin for his oddly tender and wholly sensual explorations. He pressed a kiss to the ridge of her collarbone, and then his free hand was suddenly on her knee, his fingers slipping up under the hem of her dress, curving along her thigh, and she thought about the couple on the dance floor, of what the man's hand was surely doing under the scrape of denim, and then she stopped thinking. She'd slipped into a world where everything was about feeling and wanting, and she uncrossed her legs.

A near animalistic sound tore from Chad's throat, and if it had been quieter in the club, people would've stopped to stare. Bridget's silent invitation must've had a powerful impact on him, because the grip on her lower thigh tightened, and when he kissed the space under her chin, she was scalded.

He lifted his head, and the look in his eyes did more than sear her. It caught her on fire. His hand found hers, lightly wrapping around her fingers. "I want you. I'm not going to even fuck around. I need you. Now."

And she needed him. Her entire body had turned to liquid heat, her very veins pumping molten lava to every part of her. Never before had she had such a quick response to a man.

She wet her lips with a quick swipe of her tongue, and the blue hue of his eyes churned. Her stomach was twisting into knots and dipping, plummeting.

Chad stood, his grip not leaving her hand but not tightening. He was giving her a chance to say no. He waited.

"Yes," Bridget said.

Bridget didn't remember most of the walk. All she knew was that he'd led her around the bar and down a narrow hallway she hadn't noticed before. She was surprised that he didn't take her up to one of the shady alcoves she'd seen in the front of the bar, which she was grateful for. God only knew the kind of action those places saw on a nightly basis. They ended up in a parking garage. She'd expected him to be driving something like a Porsche or Benz, but he had a new Jeep Liberty.

Displaying basic manners, he held the door open for her. Something she couldn't remember a guy doing recently. Just as she went to slide into the seat, he growled low in his throat and turned her around, pulled her into his chest, and devoured her with his mouth and lips and oh sweet baby Jesus his clever tongue. As quickly as it began though, he was stepping away and guiding her into the car. If she'd been having second thoughts, that kiss would have totally changed her mind.

Once inside, she texted Shell and said she was leaving, keeping the fact she wasn't alone to herself. Shell responded as expected. Her friend was already in the process of leaving with the guy she'd been talking to.

On the way to his house, they talked but the conversation

was strained with anticipation. Her heart was flipping out, and he kept one hand on her knee, his thumb continuously smoothing a circle along the fleshy part.

A few times, logic crept into her thoughts. She really wasn't the type of girl to get into one-night stands. At least she knew he wasn't a serial killer, but this was Chad freaking Gamble . . . and she was Bridget Rodgers, a good twenty-plus pounds curvier than a supermodel and barely able to keep her head afloat in the finance department, and he was the city's most talked about playboy with money falling out of his ears.

She was out of her league here.

And dear God, what kind of panties was she wearing tonight? The satin black ones or the granny panties? Since she hadn't seriously considered going home with someone, if it were the granny panties, she would die.

But then his thumb made another circle and her hormones beat at her logic. Pushing aside all the ways they didn't stack up together, she concentrated on the way her body was blossoming under his slight touch.

No more than twenty minutes later, Chad pulled into another parking garage. Bridget's heart jumped.

Shutting off the engine, Chad glanced at her and gave a small, secretive smile. "Ready?"

Torn between being more ready than she'd ever been and wanting to run, she nodded.

"Stay," he ordered, and then climbed out of the Jeep with an agility that made her envious. She watched him jog around the front of the car and then come to her side, opening the door. Extending an arm, he wiggled his fingers playfully.

Taking his hand, she let him pull her from the Jeep. Chad slipped an arm around her waist as he turned her toward the door. With his size and height, she actually felt small and petite for the first time in her life while tucked against his side.

They entered a wide and toasty hallway with hardwood floors. The doors with silver numbers were in dark cherry. It smelled like apples and spice in the hallway; the complete opposite of the mystery smell that clung to the cement floors and walls of what Bridget used to think was a decent apartment building she lived in.

When they stopped outside of 3307, Chad fished out his keys and opened the door. Stepping into the darkness, he flipped on a foyer light and quickly deactivated the alarm. Bridget hung back, her fingers tightening on her clutch.

The farther Chad moved in, the more lights came on. *Opulence* wasn't even a word she would use to describe his apartment. For starters, the thing was bigger than most houses in the city. Well over three thousand square feet, and the loft-style apartment was prime real estate.

The foyer led into a spacious kitchen, which was an experience in polished granite and stainless steel, double ovens and numerous cabinets. Did he cook? Bridget stole a look at Chad as he dropped his keys on the kitchen island under a rack of pans and pictured him in an apron . . . and nothing else.

He caught her stare, and his lips spread into an easy grin. "Would you like a tour?"

"I think if I see any more I'll get jealous," she admitted.

He chuckled. "But I want you to see more."

There was more to his words, an unsaid message that had the muscles in her belly tightening. She stepped forward and followed him out of the kitchen and into a formal dining room.

The long and narrow table surrounded by high-back chairs was minimalistic and gorgeous. Placed in the middle of the table was a black vase full of white flowers.

"I don't ever eat in here." Chad paused. "Okay, that's a lie. I did once when I convinced my brothers to join me for Christmas dinner."

She almost said his brothers' names but stopped herself. The image of him naked in the apron helped. "Did you cook for them?"

He arched a brow. "You sound like you'd be surprised if I said yes."

"You don't seem like the type to cook."

Chad made his way to an archway leading out of the dining area. "And what kind of man do I seem like, Bridget?"

The kind of man that would be hard if not impossible to forget after spending a night with, but she didn't say that. Bridget just shrugged, ignoring the knowing look that settled across his striking features.

The TV in the living room was grossly large, taking up almost an entire wall. A leather sectional couch and recliners formed a circle around a glass coffee table covered in sports magazines.

Chad pushed open a door underneath a spiral wooden staircase leading upstairs. "Here's my library, where I don't do a lot of reading but mostly play Angry Birds on the computer."

Bridget laughed, holding her clutch tightly as she peered around him. There were shelves lined with books, so she doubted the not-reading part unless they were there for pure looks. There were also several signed balls and mitts in glass cases hooked to the walls, mixed among encased autographed photos. It was like a baseball hall of fame up in here.

Easing the door shut, Chad nodded toward two doors beyond the staircase. "That leads to a guest bedroom and a bathroom. Upstairs?"

Her stomach flopped like she was sixteen again as she nodded, and they went upstairs. There was another bedroom used for guests, a room she soon dubbed the "white room" due to the walls, ceiling, bed, and carpet all being white. She was half afraid to step into that room.

But then he brushed past her, sliding a hand along her back as he headed down the hall, leaving a trail of hot chills in its wake. She could see down into the living room, but due to a nasty fear of heights, she backed around from the banister.

Chad nudged his bedroom door open with his hip and flipped a switch on the wall. Soft yellow light flowed across polished floors. A bed the size of a pool was in the middle of the room. He pulled a cell phone out of his pocket, tossing it carelessly onto the nightstand as if the phone didn't cost three months' worth of Bridget's rent.

Dressers that matched the headboard sat against the opposite wall, identical to the bed stands on either side of the bed. A TV hung from the wall across from the bed and a door opened to a walk-in closet that nearly brought Bridget to her knees.

"Your closet," she said, making her way to it. "I think it's the size of my bedroom."

"Originally, this was all one large room, but the interior designer built this closet and the bathroom."

The room was larger? Jesus. Her gaze traveled over the arms of dark suits and then polo shirts all color coordinated. On the shelves above, stacks of jeans—designer, no doubt—rested. Her closet at home was an extra bedroom and a bunch of cheap clothing racks. She could live in Chad's.

Knowing that the longer she stared into the closet, the more envious she'd become, she turned as Chad came up behind her, slipping an arm around her waist.

"I'm glad you said yes," he said, his warm breath dancing along her cheek. "Actually, I'm thrilled that you said yes."

Bridget tensed as heat swathed the length of her back. She turned her cheek toward him, biting down on her lower lip as his cheek grazed hers. The question blurted out of her mouth before she could stop it. "Why me?"

"Why you?" Chad pulled back a little and turned her around so that she faced him. He frowned. "I'm not sure I follow your question."

Her cheeks flushed as she tried to look away, but he caught the edge of her chin in a gentle grasp. Damn the absence of a filter. She cleared her throat. "Why did you want me to come home with you?"

Chad cocked his head to the side. "I think it's pretty obvious." His other hand slid to the curve of her hip, and he tugged her forward. She could feel him against her belly, hot and hard. "I can go into more detail if you want."

"I . . . I can tell, but you could have any girl at the club. Some of them—"

"I know I can have any woman there."

Well, he definitely wasn't lacking in the self-esteem department. "What I'm trying to say is that out of everyone there, you could've taken home one of the girls who looked like she stepped off a runway."

Chad frowned. "I did take home the one I wanted."

"But—"

"There isn't a 'but' in this." He cupped her cheek, tilting her head back. When he spoke, his lips brushed hers. "I want you. Bad. Right now. Against the wall. On my bed. The floor and maybe in the bathroom later. I have a shower stall and a Jacuzzi we could put to really good use. I know you'd like it."

Dear God . . .

His smile was pure sex. "It doesn't matter where. I want to fuck you in all those places." His lips swept across hers in a feather-light brush, and his voice dipped to a sinful whisper. "And I will."

Bridget's eyes widened—shocked by how much she enjoyed his vulgar language, but before she could respond, his mouth claimed hers in a deep, searing kiss that sparked a fire within. He pushed her back, fitting his hard body against hers. His hand left her cheek, drifting down her shoulder to the curve of her waist. And he kept kissing her—kissing her in a way a man had never kissed her before, as if he was drinking her in, taking long deep drafts, and her body melted against his. Bridget's hips tilted into him, and she was rewarded with a deep, throaty growl.

198

Lifting his head just enough that his lips left hers, he said, "Are you still confused about why I brought you home?"

"No," she breathed, dazed.

"Because I can keep showing you—actually, I want to show you." His teeth nipped at her lower lip, and her chest rose against his. "I'll admit I'm thrown off by this, too."

Second thoughts? Damn it. "You are?"

Chad nodded as both his hands landed on her hips. "Normally, I'd just get down to business. Get us off at the same time, the way we like it."

Bridget had no idea what he was talking about or how he knew the way "they liked it." All she did know was that his hands were making their way down her thighs, inching closer to the hem of her dress. Her head fell back against the wall as the tips of his fingers finally touched her bare skin.

"God, you're sexy."

Closing her eyes, her back arched, and he kissed the expanse of her bared throat as his hands slid back up her body, stopping just below her breasts. His lips found hers again, slipping his tongue inside. "I want to be inside you. All night. But I need to feel you, and then taste you first."

OBSESSION

9781473615922

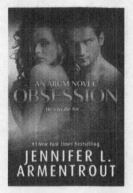

He's arrogant, domineering, and... To. Die. For.

Hunter is a ruthless killer, working for the Department of Defense. Most of the time he enjoys his job... but now he's been saddled with keeping a human from danger, and it's chafing pretty badly.

When Serena Cross witnesses her friend's murder, she's thrust into a world where her enemies would kill her to protect their otherworldly secret. Everything's topsy-turvy, and the Arum who's been sent to protect her is totally arrogant.

Hunter and Serena ignite each other's tempers even as they flee from danger – and yet, despite their differences, it seems they might be igniting one another's passion, too...

Available in ebook and paperback

HODDER

THE RETURN

9781473611573

A year ago, Seth made a deal with the gods – and pledged his life to them. Now, Apollo has a task for Seth: one which sees him playing protector over a beautiful, feisty girl who's strictly off-limits. And for someone who has a problem with restraint, this assignment might be Seth's most challenging yet.

Josie has no idea what this crazy hot guy's deal is, but he arrives in her life just as everything she's ever known is turned upside down. Either she's going insane, or a nightmare straight out of ancient myth is heading her way.

Josie can't decide which is more dangerous: an angry Titan seeking vengeance? Or the golden-eyed, secretive Seth – and the white-hot attraction developing between them...

Available in ebook and paperback

HODDER